MURDER AT THE WEDDING

CARMEL COVE COZY MYSTERY #1

M A COMLEY

JEAMEL PUBLISHING LIMITED

KEEP IN TOUCH WITH THE AUTHOR

Twitter
https://twitter.com/Melcom1

Blog
http://melcomley.blogspot.com

Facebook
http://smarturl.it/sps7jh

Newsletter
http://smarturl.it/8jtcvv

BookBub
www.bookbub.com/authors/m-a-comley

ACKNOWLEDGMENTS

Thank you as always to my rock, Jean, I'd be lost without you in my life.

Special thanks as always go to @studioenp for their superb cover design expertise.

My heartfelt thanks go to my wonderful editor Emmy Ellis, my proofreaders Joseph, Barbara and Jacqueline for spotting all the lingering nits.

OTHER BOOKS BY M A COMLEY

Blind Justice (Novella)

Cruel Justice (Book #1)

Mortal Justice (Novella)

Impeding Justice (Book #2)

Final Justice (Book #3)

Foul Justice (Book #4)

Guaranteed Justice (Book #5)

Ultimate Justice (Book #6)

Virtual Justice (Book #7)

Hostile Justice (Book #8)

Tortured Justice (Book #9)

Rough Justice (Book #10)

Dubious Justice (Book #11)

Calculated Justice (Book #12)

Twisted Justice (Book #13)

Justice at Christmas (Short Story)

Prime Justice (Book #14)

Heroic Justice (Book #15)

Shameful Justice (Book #16)

Immoral Justice (Book #17)

Toxic Justice (Book #18)

Overdue Justice (Book #19)

Unfair Justice (a 10,000 word short story)

Irrational Justice (a 10,000 word short story)

Seeking Justice (a 15,000 word novella)

Caring For Justice (a 24,000 word novella coming July 2019)

Clever Deception (co-written by Linda S Prather)

Tragic Deception (co-written by Linda S Prather)

Sinful Deception (co-written by Linda S Prather)

Forever Watching You (DI Miranda Carr thriller)

Wrong Place (DI Sally Parker thriller #1)

No Hiding Place (DI Sally Parker thriller #2)

Cold Case (DI Sally Parker thriller#3)

Deadly Encounter (DI Sally Parker thriller #4)

Lost Innocence (DI Sally Parker thriller #5)

Goodbye, My Precious Child (DI Sally Parker #6)

Web of Deceit (DI Sally Parker Novella with Tara Lyons)

The Missing Children (DI Kayli Bright #1)

Killer On The Run (DI Kayli Bright #2)

Hidden Agenda (DI Kayli Bright #3)

Murderous Betrayal (Kayli Bright #4)

Dying Breath (Kayli Bright #5)

The Hostage Takers (DI Kayli Bright Novella)

No Right to Kill (DI Sara Ramsey #1)

Killer Blow (DI Sara Ramsey #2)

The Dead Can't Speak (DI Sara Ramsey #3)

Deluded (DI Sara Ramsey #4)

The Murder Pact (DI Sara Ramsey #5)

The Caller (co-written with Tara Lyons)

Evil In Disguise – a novel based on True events

Deadly Act (Hero series novella)

Torn Apart (Hero series #1)

End Result (Hero series #2)

In Plain Sight (Hero Series #3)

Double Jeopardy (Hero Series #4)

New York Times and USA Today bestselling author M A Comley
Published by Jeamel Publishing limited
Copyright © 2019 M A Comley
Digital Edition, License Notes

CHAPTER 1

"So, Ben, you tell me. Why do people insist on getting married when they've got no intention of being faithful?"

Ruth Morgan glared at her golden Labrador for a minute, until he let out a little bark that drew her out of her thoughts.

"Yes, I know," she said. "It's not your fault my latest case found the husband guilty as all hell."

As she walked along the dirt path that wound through the long grass behind her cottage, Ruth scowled. 'Guilty as all hell' was right. The husband in question, Mr Mortimer Cummings, had been having an affair for months by the time Ruth caught him red-handed—in his office with a certain raven-haired subordinate who was definitely *not* his wife. Sure, that was her job, solving cases, but it was ones like those that upset her the most.

Spotting some tall bulrushes moving in the distance, Ben was off like a bolt, Ruth watching him wistfully. If only she could do the same to avoid this oncoming wedding. Sure, Geraldine was a dear friend, but Carmel Cove had been blabbering about her and Bradley's blasted union since the year started. So it was going to be the largest wedding Carmel Cove Hall had seen in a while, big whoop-de-do.

She couldn't put her finger on it, but for some reason, the thought of the wedding filled her with a cold creepy feeling of dread.

Maybe it was how the whole thing was bound to be the height of extravagance—Lady Falkirk would allow no less at her not-so-humble abode. When she'd offered Carmel Cove Hall to the happy couple for their wedding, they'd found themselves unable to refuse.

"Are you sulking about the wedding again?"

Hearing James' voice, Ruth turned around, her scowl defiant. "No."

"Good." James hooked his arm through hers. "Since I'm the one who should be sulking. More people who've been together way less than us are getting married."

"Don't," Ruth said. "Carolyn already laid into me when I told her I was wearing my pants suit to the wedding."

James chuckled, although he patted her arm consolingly. "Carolyn would."

"She's all la-la over the wedding, too," Ruth said darkly, thinking back to the way her sister had condemned her attitude regarding her best friend's wedding. "She called me a damn pessimist."

James said nothing—he knew better than to light the fire of Ruth's ire. But it was too late. That fire was lit—and blazing.

"If you saw as many relationships as I have crash and burn over the years, then you'd be pessimistic, too," she replied simply.

She didn't add the other part—the one that pertained to them. After being together for the past decade, James had upped the ante in the last two years, done everything bar getting down on one knee to plead with her to 'get hitched'. Although Ruth's excuses ran the gamut, she'd never admitted the real reason to her boyfriend behind her not wanting to commit that heavily into their relationship. It wasn't that she didn't care for him, nothing could be further from the truth; if anything she cared for him too deeply. Plain and simple, and probably silly, but there it was. Ten years was a hell of a long time and, by now, James was woven as intricately into Ruth's life as Ben. She didn't want to risk changing things or losing what they had now by 'upgrading' their relationship. Besides, they were happy now—what was the rush?

The long grass rustled, and Ben came racing back, a stick prominently held in his proud jaws. Ruth and James crouched to give his golden head a good scratch.

"Good boy," Ruth said.

Taking the stick, she threw it, and Ben was off. She and James watched him bounding through the grass without a care in the world.

"If only Ben could come along to the wedding," Ruth mused, a slight smile on her face. "Then things would really be interesting."

"I'm sure they'll be interesting either way," James pointed out. "The whole town will be there, you know."

Ruth smirked. "Oh, believe me, I know."

THAT NIGHT, the phone rang. James answered it and called out for her to pick up the extension. Ruth was knee-deep in admin duties that she hadn't had time to complete at the office the past week. She snatched at it and said distractedly, "Our pipes don't need to be cleaned."

"Am I not allowed to call my best friend the night before my wedding?" Geraldine asked in a half-joking, half-hurt tone.

"Sorry," Ruth said. "James didn't say it was you."

"Maybe he didn't recognise my voice," Geraldine said, sounding stressed. "I'm freaking out over here."

"It is a big day. One of the biggest you're likely to see unless you walk down the aisle numerous times."

"Oi, there's no need to say that. Condemning our marriage before it's even begun."

"I did nothing of the sort. I was merely stating facts. Do you have any idea the number of marriages that end up in the divorce courts? Anyway, it was your choice to get married, nothing you can do to change that now, especially within the next twenty-four hours." Ruth rubbed Ben behind his ears. He moaned softly, enjoying the unexpected attention.

"Crap, what the heck has got into you?"

"Sorry, just one of those days, and no, it's not that time of the month before you ask. What's up?"

"I have doubts and I need to run them past someone. I thought you'd be that person. I'm not so sure now."

"Doubts? Are you *crazy?*"

"I know, right? The big day five years in the making. I mean, five years is long enough to really know someone, isn't it?"

Ruth paused. "Why do you ask? What aspect are you concerned about exactly?"

"Everything. I'm worried that my dress won't fit, or I'll trip, or Bradley will trip or will forget to show up."

"Are you *kidding* me? You're nuts! It's your wedding day. He won't forget. Besides, he adores you."

That much was clear to anyone who had eyes. Bradley doted on Geraldine, apparently buying her roses every week, chocolates every month. He was the poster child for a good partner, as James was keen on saying every time he tried buying Ruth roses or chocolates and she turned them down.

"You're right," Geraldine said, sounding better already. "Although the whole Caribbean honeymoon is stressful, too. I'm not one hundred percent packed yet as I can't decide what to pack."

"Well, you know what I'd recommend."

"I'm *not* packing a trouser suit or jeans," Geraldine said. "You know me."

"Yes," Ruth said. "You love citrus-coloured skirts and dresses as much as I hate them. Pack a trillion of them then."

"Gee, thanks. Some help you are."

"You're welcome."

A pause, then the two women laughed. "Really, though," Geraldine said. "You're right, I'm just being silly." She let out a loud sigh. "I just need some camomile tea and a lie-down. Choosing a dress be damned!"

"That's more like it," Ruth said, smiling. "You'll do great tomorrow."

"Thanks, Ruth. I'm sure everything will be all right with you by my side. Have I told you lately how much I love you?"

"Not lately, but I'm aware. Let's hope things don't change between us once Bradley slips the ring on your finger." It was another reason why Ruth was reluctant to walk down the aisle, in case James changed and became more demanding of her time. At the moment she did what she wanted and when. All that could change in the blink of an eye and with a band of gold, just like it had with a few of her other friends over the years.

"They won't, I promise you. Goodnight."

"Sleep well. See you bright and early in the morning." Geraldine had pleaded with her to be a bridesmaid, but Ruth turned down the invitation. She had to—there was no way she'd be seen dead wearing a girly pastel dress overlaid in itchy lace. The rejection had caused a slight rift between her and Geraldine for a few months until Geraldine found it in her heart to forgive her.

When she put down the phone, Ruth couldn't figure out what was sitting uncomfortably with her, but it was there all the same. That distinctive chill of foreboding, like the stroke of one icy finger down her spine…

RUTH STRETCHED out the knots in her back when she woke the next morning in the spare room, needing matchsticks for her eyes. After desperately trying to sleep and failing miserably, James had pleaded with her to let him sleep and asked her to leave the room—either that or he was willing to spend the night on the couch. She eventually buckled around three a.m. and slipped into the spare room. Ben jumped on the bed to join her for a cuddle. She was keen to feel his warmth because she was still feeling decidedly chilly—bizarre, considering the time of year, the first week in July.

"Knock, knock. I thought I'd bring you breakfast in bed. How did you sleep?" James was the epitome of a man who'd had a carefree night's sleep. He was freshly shaven, his hair damp from the shower, wearing the silk robe she'd given him the previous Christmas. He placed the tray with eggs, bacon and sausage down on the bed beside her and shooed Ben from his comfy position.

Ruth ran a hand over her flat tummy. She wasn't sure she'd want something so heavy first thing, not the way her tummy was churning. "It's really kind of you, James, especially after how annoying I was last night. I just don't know if I've got the stomach for anything other than a slice of toast this morning."

He placed a pillow against the leather headboard and removed the tray then fell into position beside her. "I thought you might say that. I only made the one breakfast just in case. All right if I tuck in?"

She should have been angry with him, but she wasn't. She was used to the wacky way he thought now and again. Maybe he knew her better than she knew herself at times. She leaned over and kissed him as he plunged a heavily loaded forkful of the ingredients from the plate into his mouth.

"What was that for?" he asked, his words barely audible through the food filling his cheeks.

"Because, no matter how much you tick me off at times, and believe me, you do, I still love you." He opened his mouth to speak, baring the contents. She held up her hand to prevent him from spitting his food across the clean bed linen. "And before you say it, no, that is not giving you the green light to ask me to marry you for the seven thousandth time."

He shook his head, disappointment pulling at his features. In between emptying his mouth and shovelling in the next forkful, he said, with sad puppy-dog eyes, "Hopefully you'll change your mind one day."

Ruth swept back the quilt, tucking it alongside him, and hopped out of bed into her fluffy slippers. "Maybe, when I'm old and grey." That comment was usually enough to put an end to the irritating conversation. A twinge pained her heart for treating him so badly— not that she was, she loved him, it was the thought of mentioning the M-word that made her constantly break out in a cold sweat that soured her mood.

She looked back over her shoulder and blew him a kiss. "I love you, babe, just not ready to commit. You know how much this wedding is getting on my nerves. I adore Geraldine, you know that, but I've had as much as I can stand for one year with wedding plans."

He placed his cutlery on the plate and sighed. "Sorry if you think I'm bugging you all the time. Aren't weddings supposed to bring out the romance in people?"

Ruth grunted and walked out of the bedroom and shouted, "Not me. Can't stand them. They're a waste of money. It costs thousands to get hitched properly. That money could be invested in a couple's first home together."

James' silence was deafening, leading her to wonder if she'd gone too far this time. She hopped in the shower and spent the next five minutes going over their discussion in her head until a recent conversation she'd had with her own mother lately resurfaced. 'That boy loves the very bones of you—Lord knows why, when you treat him like dirt most of the time. It wouldn't surprise me if he runs off and leaves you high and dry one day.' Her mother's harsh words had shaken her to the core at the time. She had never treated James badly, not to her knowledge. He knew deep down how much she loved him, even if she didn't demonstrate it that much. She had never regarded herself as a heart-and-flowers type of girl.

After showering, she returned to the bedroom. Her heart sank when she found the bed empty. *See, that just proves how much I love him, doesn't it?*

The wedding was due to take place at eleven, although Geraldine had pleaded with her to show up early to help prepare her for her big day, something Ruth had grudgingly agreed to do despite Geraldine having a grown-up bridesmaid on the day. She would need to be at Carmel Cove Hall at nine-thirty. "Not a minute late!" her best friend had warned her. Ruth had gained a reputation of showing up to events of this magnitude a little late over the years.

She strained her neck, trying to hear what James was up to. Nothing. No, wait, there, in the distance, she could faintly make out the clash of plates and pots and pans. Bless him, he was washing up for her. *Why shouldn't he? He made the damn mess!*

Ruth towel-dried her long red hair then brushed it, screeching a few times as the brush hit the odd knot at the end. *Maybe I should cut it all off and have a bob instead. It would save going through all this hassle every other day.* She knew she would do no such thing; she loved having long curly hair, it was a statement. She might reject the possibility to dress girlie, but it didn't mean she had to go around wearing short hair. Lots of women preferred to wear trousers and jeans, didn't they?

She turned to ask Ben's opinion. "Long or short, bubsy?"

He offered her his paw. She lowered herself to kiss it, and Ben let out a satisfied moan. He was with her twenty-four-seven, the only constant in her life. He went to work with her at the office and even travelled in the car next to her when she ventured out on her covert investigations for clients. The two of them made up the entire staff of the Carmel Cove Detective Agency. She was proud of her achievements. The business was now in its fifth year and going from strength to strength. More and more clients were showing up at her door. This year was going to be her best to date, both in the number of cases she'd solved and in the reimbursements she'd received from clients, praising her for a job well done. She had taken over the agency from Frank Warren who had retired due to ill health. Judging by the state in which he'd left the office in and the amount of full-size whisky bottles —empty bottles—she'd discovered in the numerous drawers in her desk, she suspected he had liver problems, in that it was probably pickled and wrinkled after all these years of alcohol abuse.

Ruth glanced over at the clock. It was already ten minutes after eight, and she hadn't even dried her hair yet. She pecked Ben on the nose. He whimpered again and cutely used his paw to rub the spot her lips had touched. "I must get on." He remained seated on the floor beside her, raising his head when she dried the opposite side, enjoying the warm breeze from the drier on his face. Ruth smiled. He was such an adorable dog, not a bad bone in his body. She felt sad that he'd have to spend long hours cooped up in the house today while she and James attended this damn wedding.

There it was again, the W-word, a constant reminder, poking her with a stick.

After drying her hair, she stood and shook the pins and needles out of her legs, regretting that she'd chosen to dry her hair on the floor instead of using the seat tucked under the pretty dressing table James had lovingly restored for her a few months earlier.

She opened her wardrobe door. Everything was lined up according to colour—pale colours to the left and the warmer, darker colours on the right. She ran her fingers along the lighter end and plucked out the cream linen suit she'd treated herself to from the local boutique. She knew, as soon as she had laid eyes on it in the window, that she'd have to own it. It had cost her a packet, over five hundred, but James had encouraged her to purchase it. He'd even chipped in a couple of hundred of his hard-earned cash to see the smile on her face when she'd tried it on in the boutique. There was no hesitation once the lush material had slithered over her skin. She'd played the 'I can't afford it' card, and that was when James had offered to stump up the rest of the cash.

She laid the trouser suit out on the bed and went to the other end of the wardrobe, where she plucked out the red blouse she'd bought a few weeks later when her bank balance had been regenerated. The contrast made it a winning combination, in her eyes anyway.

Ruth turned her attention to her makeup. She withdrew the stool from its hiding place, sat at the dressing table and riffled though the drawer next to her, picking out the colours she wanted to wear. She chose a subtle palette for the occasion, highlighted her vivid green eyes with a shimmering gold on her lids and applied thin, black strokes of mascara to her lashes. She had no need to slather on any foundation because the weather in the cove had been stunning so far during the summer. Her usually pale skin had turned a light golden brown within weeks. Nevertheless, she took out her bulky brush and applied a couple of lines of blusher along her cheekbones. Admiring her skills, she smiled and nodded at her reflection. "You'll do."

Time was flying past this morning, and she'd soon need to complete her appearance by slipping on her blouse and suit. She was conscious of waiting until the last minute, trying to avoid any unnecessary creases before she set off. Which was foolish really, because once she got behind the steering wheel of her car, she knew the creases would appear.

"I need to visit the loo. All the washing up is done, no need for you to get grubby this morning," James shouted out.

"Eww…too much information. You're an angel. Thanks, James."

He chuckled "Yeah, I know, what would you do without me?"

The door to the bathroom closed. She studied her reflection. "What would I do indeed? So why not marry the poor man?" She shrugged and left the dressing table again.

After carefully slipping into her suit and blouse, she slid on the navy-blue high heels she'd bought to enhance her ensemble and picked up the matching clutch bag she'd had for a few years, then walked downstairs to the kitchen, ensuring Ben went before her in case he caught her and she ended up in a heap at the bottom. That would be a travesty after the effort she'd put in to getting ready.

She heard the latch on the bathroom door open and James thud across the floor to their bedroom above. "James, I'm going to shoot off now. I'll see you later. Will you ensure Ben does his business in the back garden before you leave? I'd hate to come home to a mess."

"You worry too much. He'll be fine. Go, enjoy yourself. Send my love to Geraldine, and I'll see you later."

CHAPTER 2

ON THE DRIVE through the quaint harbourside town she'd called home since her parents had moved here when she was ten, she could feel the buzz and excitement emanating from its inhabitants. It was the start of summer. A smattering of tourists had already flocked to the area. They were lucky. Carmel Cove was never really what you'd call inundated with 'grockels' as the locals preferred to call them. There was the odd Bed and Breakfast dotted around the town and a hotel up on the coastal path, but apart from that there was nowhere else to house them. Thankfully, none of the local farmers had sold off any of their land for someone to start up one of those godawful glamping sites that appeared to be in trend nowadays.

There were several campsites on the outskirts of the next village of Lunder, but the campers who frequented them rarely came into town. Those who did venture in generally behaved themselves. They'd feel the wrath of the townsfolk if they didn't. That was the type of place Carmel Cove was, friendly, with a couple of hundred inhabitants, out of the few thousand, you could count on whenever trouble struck. Apart from the odd few who Ruth had fallen out with over the years, everyone was jolly and mindful of giving the other inhabitants the space they needed to live their lives unscathed.

She waved to Denis Makey, the local butcher, who also happened to be the husband of one of her dear friends, Hilary. She pulled over and lowered the window to chat to him. "Hi, Denis, I bet you're busy."

"I am, Ruth. It's all right having these weddings going on in the town, but when you're the only butcher around for miles…well, you can imagine what the workload has been like this week. Still, I mustn't complain, it's cash in the till at the end of the day."

"That's right. I'd better fly. I have a jittery bride to calm down at the other end. I'll see you at the reception later, yes?"

"Much later. I'm on my way up there to drop off some goodies now, but I'll be going through the trade entrance."

They both laughed at the way he'd said the last two words. A posh voice really didn't suit him one iota. He was such a down-to-earth, lovable character.

"See you there. Tell Hilary I've got something to share with her later that could be beneficial to both of us."

"Sounds secretive. Anything I should be worried about? You won't be discussing how to bump me off, will you?" He winked and covered his heart with his hand.

"I'd hardly likely to give you any hints if that were the case, would I now?" Ruth laughed, pressed the button to close the window and continued on her journey.

The road wound through the coastal town and up the hill. Halfway up, she indicated right and turned into the long sweeping drive of the historic mansion where her best friend had been given the chance to wed her beloved. Ruth sighed as the grand honey-coloured stone house emerged from the trees shielding it from nosy parkers hoping to catch a gander from the main road.

Dozens of vehicles were lined up along one side of the gravelled drive. There was a small marquee erected on the lawn off to the left, waiters and waitresses rushing in and out, dressed in black and white. She could imagine the view from above, the serving staff looking and acting like worker ants on a mission.

No wonder Geraldine was stressed out with all this going on. She would've organised the whole shebang. There was no way on earth that Bradley would've offered to lend a hand. He was one of those people who soaked in the glory of other people's hard work and organisational skills. Of course, that might be her just having a downer on men at the moment. *Get a grip, girl. Leave the poor buggers alone.*

She removed the large wedding present, that James had pitched in with, from the back seat and locked the car door. Every step she took, with the heavy present, she pondered whether Geraldine would appreciate the effort they'd gone to when choosing the dinner service she was about to present to her. It was nothing fancy, mostly a plain cream with a splash of colour in the form of a blue butterfly on the side of the dishes. She shrugged. If Geraldine hated it then Ruth would be more than happy to use it at home, so no big deal.

The butler approached her. "Yes, can I help you?"

"I'm the bride's best friend, Ruth. She's expecting me."

"Ah yes, I didn't recognise you, Miss."

Meaning what? That I've scrubbed up well and that I usually look like the dregs of society in my daily life?

Ruth smiled tautly. "I bet you say that to all the girls."

"Actually, I don't," he replied, no hint of a smile. "I'll show you upstairs. The bride is using one of the guest bedrooms to get ready for the occasion."

"Thank you." *No, it's fine, I can manage, don't put yourself out offering to help.*

He walked ahead of her, his steps slow and steady as they ascended the grandest staircase Ruth had ever had the privilege of using. "Is everything ready?"

"Nearly. Just a few tweaks to add here and there. Maybe you can pass that on to the bride. She came out of the room about half an hour ago in a right tizzy."

"Only natural I suppose. She wants the day to go off without a hitch."

He continued up the stairs and knocked on the first door on his right. It was opened swiftly by Geraldine—perhaps she was expecting to have to sort out yet another problem that had arisen.

"My God, where have you been? You're late as usual."

Ruth glanced at her gold watch, another gift from the man desperate to marry her, and sighed. "Two minutes. Hey, that's good for me, and you know it is."

"Yes, yes. Get in here." Geraldine grabbed her wrist and yanked her into the room. "Couldn't you have left the gift downstairs?"

"Thanks, I love your dress, too," Ruth replied, smarting that Geraldine hadn't noticed the effort she'd put in for her best friend's wedding.

Geraldine placed her hand to her cheek. "I'm so sorry. What a dunderhead I am. You look gorgeous, darling."

The bridesmaid, Carol, stepped forward with a smile and relieved Ruth of the present. "Hi, Ruth. I'm so glad you're here." She rolled her eyes as if emphasising the truth behind her statement.

"Has she been a pain in the rear? A bridezilla?" Carol and Ruth laughed while Geraldine's mouth dropped open, revealing several fillings at the back of her mouth. "Wow, someone overdosed on sugar when they were younger." Ruth chuckled at the nonplussed expression that swept across Geraldine's face.

"What the heck is that supposed to mean? I swear you're in a world of your own at times, where only you know what you're talking about," Geraldine chastised her. She stomped across the room and stood in the huge bay window, gazing out, surveying what was going on below them.

"Come away from the window, it'll only stress you out more. Everything is going according to plan."

Geraldine swivelled to face her and crossed her arms. "How in the dickens would you know that?"

"I can tell. There was no one shouting when I arrived or pulling chunks of hair out. Just calm down. You look amazing by the way. Beautiful and majestic one might even say."

Geraldine unfolded her arms, lightly touched the dress at her thighs and spun around on the spot. "I feel like a princess. Hey, you should try it one day."

Ruth shook her head. "Nice try. Don't get me started. One posh wedding a year is all this town can handle, I reckon."

"Does that mean that you'll be walking down the aisle with James next year then?"

"No, and stop twisting my words. What's left to do before the celebrant arrives to m...marry you?" she asked, struggling in her attempt to say the M-word.

"I'm ready. I have been for the past hour."

Ruth shook her head. "That was pretty dumb of you."

"Why?"

"Because you're going to be a long time on your feet today. You should have made the most of it this morning. Now you won't be able to sit down, not unless you want to crease your sumptuous dress in the process."

"I'm well aware of that now. Thank you for pointing out the obvious in your own inimitable way."

"Calm down. I was joking. Gosh, don't go losing your sense of humour on me now, not this late in the day."

There was a slight tap on the door. As Ruth was the nearest, she rushed to open it. She smiled when she saw the elegant woman standing in the doorway. It was Geraldine's mother.

"Is she here?"

Ruth swept to the side so Valerie could see her beautiful daughter, the sun shining behind her, making her look serene and angelic.

"Oh, Geraldine. You look stunning."

"Don't cry, Mum, you'll start me off, and Carol has spent the last half an hour perfecting my makeup. Where's Dad?"

"He's downstairs, ensuring the bar is set up properly."

"You mean he's propping it up as usual. Couldn't he behave himself just for one day?" Sadness descended and clouded Geraldine's previously happy face.

"Now, love. Let him be. He likes a tipple now and again, there's no harm in that. Especially on an auspicious occasion such as this. Don't begrudge him having a good time."

Geraldine's smiley face turned upside down as if a storm was brewing within her.

Ruth was desperate to ease the conversation in a different direction, aware of how upset Geraldine could get about her father's drinking. "When do you set off on honeymoon, love?"

Geraldine's dreamy smile returned. "Later this evening. I think I'm more excited about that than the actual wedding."

Ruth shook her head. "I doubt that's true. I'm so happy for you."

They hugged gently, not wishing to crush the bridal gown.

"Thank you, that truly means a lot. I know you and Bradley have never really seen eye to eye on certain subjects," Geraldine said.

"He can't help being an ass seventy-five percent of the time."

Geraldine roared. "I won't tell him you said that. He makes me happy, happier than I've ever been in my life. I know I'd be lost without him. He feels the same way about me."

"I should hope so after going to all this bother. You deserve any happiness coming your way, sweetheart. I may be a grouch sometimes when the subject of marriage rears its ugly head, but I appreciate not everyone shares the same views as me on the subject."

"You know James is desperate to tie the knot, don't you?"

"I know. He's also aware how much I love him without the need to commit fully to him."

"Are you sure he'll be willing to hang around in the future if you insist on being stubborn?"

She stared at Geraldine. "Is that a likely possibility?"

"In my day, you never kept a man hanging around for too long. He'd be off, chasing another piece of skirt if he wasn't satisfied at home," Valerie piped up.

Geraldine placed a hand on top of Ruth's. "I don't think Mum meant it like that."

"Oh, didn't I?" her mother snapped unnecessarily. "Men think with that thing dangling between their legs far more often than women perceive."

"Mother, will you please give it a rest? Ruth and James have a solid relationship. It's entirely up to them how they handle it going forward."

"I was just saying."

"Well don't. Why don't you go and make sure Dad doesn't drink the bar dry before the other guests arrive?"

Her mother's back went rigid. "Well, that's a nice way to talk about your father. Okay, I know where I'm not wanted. I'll see you downstairs—that is if I don't get a better offer in the meantime." Her mother stomped out of the room and slammed the door behind her.

Ruth took a step towards Geraldine who had tears welling up. "She'll calm down soon, she always does."

"I'm dreading what will happen during the wedding. If Dad makes a show of me on my big day, I'll never be able to forgive him. His drinking has got a lot worse lately since he lost his job. You'd think he'd be hanging on to his money; instead, he's spending it as if it were water, on anything but water. Makes me so sad. I have a sneaky suspicion he's hit Mum once or twice in recent weeks, too, all because of the dreaded drink."

Ruth gasped. "You're kidding! How can your mother sit back and defend him like that?"

"I asked her the same question. Her response is always that she *lurves* him. Gosh, am I really doing the right thing? What if Bradley gets comfortable with our relationship and starts taking me for granted the way Dad does to Mum?"

"He won't. Your parents' relationship will have no bearing on what lies ahead of you and Bradley in the future. If he ever steps out of line, he knows he'll have me to deal with."

"Gosh, I think he'd run for the hills if that were the case."

In the far corner of the room, Carol, who had been keeping herself busy, gasped.

"What's wrong, Carol?" Geraldine flew across the room, concerned.

Carol's cheeks were flushed when she turned to face them. "Oh nothing, just me being silly. I thought I saw one of my exes arrive with one of my best friends."

17

"Who? Jeff?" Geraldine asked.

"Yeah, was he invited?" Carol inclined her head.

"Sorry, yes. He's a friend of Bradley's. I couldn't say no when he suggested he wanted him to come. I didn't think of the implications. Do you want me to have a word? Tell him to go home?"

Carol rubbed Geraldine's arm. "Don't be daft. It's just me being me. I'll be all right by the time we go downstairs. Not long to go now. We should be running through our countdown list, make sure we haven't forgotten anything."

Ruth smiled, admiring Carol's courage in the situation, not sure if she'd be able to put up with an ex showing up with his new bit of stuff on his arm who just happened to be her best friend. But then, none of Ruth's friends would ever do such an atrocious thing to her, would they? "Do you want me to leave you to it?"

"There's no need for you to go. I need you here to help keep my nerves at bay. I can't believe there's only half an hour to go before I say 'I do'."

"How are your nerves? You seem pretty calm to me."

Geraldine held her hand out in front of her. It was as steady as a rock. "So far so good, in spite of my falling out with mother."

"It was hardly a falling out. A few home truths maybe. I'm sure she'll be fine when you breeze down the grand staircase and up the aisle." Ruth smiled reassuringly. "Why don't I get us all a nice cup of coffee?"

"That would be great," Carol was the first to reply, nodding appreciatively.

"I'll be back in a tick." Ruth left the room and stood at the top of the staircase, surveying all the townsfolk who'd been lucky enough to receive an invite, milling into the hallway below. The inhabitants of the town had done her friend proud, all of them dressed up for the occasion in their finer clothes, suits for the men and a mixture of dresses and trouser suits for the ladies. She let out a relieved sigh, knowing she wouldn't be the only woman wearing trousers today. However, she hit herself in the thigh when she realised she'd forgotten to purchase a hat for the occasion. *Numpty, why didn't I think of getting a hat?* She had a good excuse for that, at least that was what she told herself. She'd been snowed under with work for the past few weeks. Work that had seen her putting in fourteen- and fifteen-hour days, hardly giving her time to sleep, let alone go hat shopping.

She was still annoyed the thought had slipped her mind.

A wolf whistle sounded below her. She scanned the crowd through narrowed eyes, hating it when she passed by builders in the street who dared to do that within range of her. She smiled when she realised James was standing at the bottom of the stairs, waiting for her. She glided down the staircase towards him, feeling like Krystle Carrington out of *Dynasty* in her salubrious surroundings.

James greeted her with a proud grin and leaned forward to peck her on the cheek. "I'm the envy of most men in this room. You look stunning, my love."

Never one to take compliments when they were offered, she swiped the top of his arm and whispered, "You're biased."

He laughed and tucked her arm through his. "Maybe a little. How's the bride?"

"Fair to middling." She unhitched herself. "I've only come down for a few coffees. Where am I likely to get some, do you think?"

"My guess would be the marquee. I'll go and chase some down for you, if you like?"

"Would you mind?"

"Where are you? I'll bring them up when I've managed to locate some."

"The first door at the top of the stairs. Can we have three cups, all white?"

"I'll bring them up in a second." James rushed through the throng of guests and out into the garden, acting like a puppy eager to please.

Another stab of guilt jabbed her in the stomach. She turned and walked back up the stairs and into the room. "James came to my rescue. He's gone to track some down, he shouldn't be long." She wagged her finger when Geraldine opened her mouth to speak. "Don't go there. I know that look. Leave things well alone if you value our friendship."

"That's a tad harsh. My lips are sealed. Except to say, what an absolute treasure you have on your hands in James."

"Right, what's left to do, Carol?" Ruth quickly changed the subject, not for the first time that day.

"The bouquet, I need to chase that up. It should have been delivered by now. I'll be back in a jiffy."

When Carol left the room, Geraldine was quick to point out, "You would've had that organised first thing this morning, wouldn't you?"

"More than likely. She's still done an amazing job keeping you in check. Sorry you fell out with your mum, love. Try not to let that spoil your day."

Geraldine wafted a hand in front of her. "It's forgotten about. I just hope Dad behaves himself. The odds are against me on that one. He's really been an utter swine recently. You know he refused to pay towards the wedding, don't you? Bradley and I had to get a loan to pay for all this. I was so grateful to Lady Falkirk for giving us the opportunity to use this place for the venue. She's refusing to take any money for the privilege."

Ruth's mouth hung open for a second or two. "I had no idea. Why didn't you confide in me? I would have helped out where I could, you know that."

"I didn't want to burden you with the truth. That's why it's been such a stressful time for me the last few months. Up until the time Dad was still in work, my parents said they were going to foot the bill for everything. When Dad dropped the bombshell, I either had to get the loan or cancel the wedding altogether."

"Oh, sweetheart, that must've been tough for you to deal with. I hope Bradley has helped in some way?"

"He agreed to go halves on the loan. He needn't have, but he has."

"Why didn't you just elope? No one would have blamed you. Now you're saddled with debt before your married life has begun. Is it truly worth it?"

Geraldine sighed. "I think so. This is what I've always dreamed of, Ruth. I know how excessive you think all of this is, but it's been my dream since I was a little girl, to have a full-scale, over-the-top wedding."

"I don't blame you if you've had that dream for the last thirty years, love. Hey, is your father giving you away?"

"Yes, he's supposed to be, which is why I went off on one earlier. What if he shows me up? How the hell is it going to look on the wedding photos if he's drunk?"

"Do you want me to have a word with him, ensure that doesn't happen?"

"No, don't you dare. It'll probably make him worse."

"All right. I'll keep an eye on him. Maybe I can have a word with the barman, tell him to water down his drinks somehow. My friend used to have a problem with her husband being an alcoholic and making a show of her. She used to run vodka around the rim of the glass and fill it up with tonic. It fooled him for a while. It might work on your father, too."

"It's worth a try."

Carol entered the room with the bride's bouquet in her hand, a visual display of perfect pinks and lilacs interspersed with white, matching Carol's bridesmaid's dress to perfection.

Geraldine teared up.

"Don't cry. You're going to spoil your mascara," Ruth warned, whipping out a tissue from her clutch bag sitting on the luxurious chair close to the bed.

"It's beautiful. Thanks, Carol. What about the other two brides-maids, are they here yet? Donna said she would get them ready at home. She thought it would be less hassle that way."

"They've just arrived. Donna was busy chasing them around downstairs. She said she'd round them up and be with us in a few minutes."

"That's a relief. I was wondering where they were. I hope they keep their dresses clean, at least until after the ceremony."

"I think that's Donna's intention." Carol sniggered.

There was a knock on the door. Ruth shot across the room and eased it open a little to see who the caller was. She opened it fully.

James stood there with three cups and saucers sitting on a silver tray. "Just in time, thanks for this, love."

He glanced over Ruth's shoulder and let out a low whistle. "Wow, wow, wow. Geraldine, you look absolutely beautiful. Simply stunning."

Geraldine curtsied. "Why thank you, kind sir. I hope Bradley approves."

"Are you nuts? Of course he will. There'd have to be something seriously wrong with him if he didn't. Right, I'll get off then and leave you to it. Holler if you need anything else."

Ruth stepped into the hallway and kissed him full on the lips.

"Wow. I'll have to bring you coffee more often if that's how you're going to show your appreciation."

"I just wanted to let you know how much I love you. Maybe it's wedding fever. Don't go getting any ideas, though, for now."

He tilted his head. "So there still is hope for us walking down the aisle?"

"Of course there is. Enough about our futile dilemma, I need you to do me a favour. Ask the barman to play around with Geraldine's father's drinks, if you would. He's been hitting the bottle lately; I'll fill you in with all the details after the wedding. He's giving her away, and she's concerned he'll be blotto during the wedding photos. Let's see if we can avoid that."

"Leave it with me. Can I get another one of those kisses?"

She kissed him long and hard. "There, now shoo, you have an important job to do."

"Anything for you."

Ruth smiled and pushed him on his way. Parched, she returned to the room and headed for the tray of drinks. She raised her cup. "To Geraldine and Bradley, may this day be like no other."

Geraldine tittered and touched Ruth's forehead. "That's pretty profound for you. Are you feeling all right?"

"Ha, and you wonder why I refused to be your bridesmaid." She winked at Carol, and they all laughed.

"Thank you for being here with us and for all your valuable friendship over the years. I would have been lost without you by my side on numerous occasions. So what if you turned me down on my special day, I'll never hold that against you. I might fling it in your face now and again if we have a tiff though."

"That sounds about right. Let's sup up and make the final moments of your single life full of laughter and cheer, because it's going to be all downhill from here, lady."

"You never give up. I'll make you eat your words."

Ruth took her cup over to the window and gazed out at the crowd gathering below.

"I have to admit that I'm getting a little nervous now," Geraldine said, joining her.

"You'll be fine. The ceremony will be over before you know it, not like the one I attended in France."

Geraldine frowned. "Why? How long was that?"

"Four *long* hours. My bum was numb after a couple of hours, and my legs tingled with pins and needles. To crown it all, I couldn't understand a damn word that was being said."

"Oh my. That would be pure torture for me, not speaking the lingo. You poor thing."

"Much prefer a celebrant's wedding, far less formal. You did the right thing, love."

"I hope so." Geraldine sighed heavily.

After they'd finished their drinks, they spent the next five minutes ensuring everything was in place. "Right, I'm going to do some organising downstairs now. Wishing you luck. I'll speak to you after the ceremony. Try and keep the nerves to a minimum. Love you lots."

"Thank you, Ruth. For everything, but most of all for being the best friend a girl could have. Even if your sarcastic wit took an eternity to get used to."

Ruth laughed and hugged her lightly. "Take care of her, Carol. I'll send the little munchkins up."

"She's in safe hands, don't worry."

Ruth left the room, an anxious knot lying in the pit of her stomach for some reason. From her observation point at the top of the grand staircase, she spotted the two bridesmaids causing havoc among the other guests, and their mother failing miserably to keep them under control.

She swept down the stairs and straight towards them. "Hello, Donna. Are these two adorable creatures causing mischief as usual?"

"Hi, Ruth. You could say that. I was hoping to lessen their enthusiasm for the day by keeping them at home longer. I guess that didn't work out too well."

"Want me to round them up? Geraldine would like a word with them about their roles before the ceremony begins."

"We'll do it together."

Ruth set off in one direction while Donna circulated the crowd from the other. Within seconds they were working like a sheepdog and its master, rounding up his flock. "Tilly and Milly, I've got you."

The five-year-olds tried their hardest to free themselves from Ruth's tight grip. She had no intention of letting them go. Donna arrived and chastised her children.

"You've let me down, girls. You promised me you'd behave today. Have you forgotten this is a special occasion? It's not all about you. Now, go with Ruth. She'll take you upstairs to where Auntie Geraldine is getting ready. This is serious stuff now. Any messing about from this moment on, and I will start dishing out punishment. No TV for a week, and that's just for starters. Do I make myself clear?"

"Yes, Mummy. We're sorry, Mummy. We pwomise to be good from now on," one of the twins said, although Ruth wasn't sure which one.

"Come on, you two. Upstairs with you. Time's marching on, and the wedding is about to start."

The twins grinned broadly, and they both slipped a hand into Ruth's outstretched ones. Ruth led them slowly up the stairs, both of them lifting their skirts during the journey.

"We've never been bwidesmaids before. What do we have to do, Ruth?"

"Geraldine will run through what's expected of you in a moment. Just be yourselves, cute, and most of all, have fun."

"We can do that, can't we, Milly?"

"We can, Tilly. It's going to be a lot of fun. I'm weally looking forward to it."

"Good. It should be a day you never forget. Hey, if you show all the guests how well you can behave, maybe, just maybe, they'll be lining up to have you at their weddings as bridesmaids. How about that?" Ruth said, resisting the urge to replace the R in *bridesmaid* like Tilly had.

The girls were exhausted after their exploits and the steep climb up the staircase. They made a beeline for the bed the second Ruth opened the door.

Geraldine gasped. "Oh, my goodness. Girls, come here, you look adorable. Give me a twirl."

Reluctantly, the girls slipped off the bed again and circled slowly, one going left to right and the other twin choosing to rotate in the opposite direction.

"Don't they look beautiful, Ruth and Carol?" Geraldine gushed.

"They do indeed. Like fairy princesses," Carol replied, reaching forward and fluffing out the girls' dresses after they'd crushed them sitting on the bed.

"Okay. I'm going to wish you good luck for the second time and love you and leave you. Knock them dead, gorgeous. I'm so proud of what you've achieved in such a short time. It's going to be the best and most memorable wedding this town has ever seen."

"Thank you, Ruth. That means a lot. See you later."

Ruth left the room and shuddered, not liking the sudden chill that swept through her. She rubbed at the goose bumps springing to life on her arms as she surveyed the crowd from the top of the staircase once more. She spotted James talking to Geraldine's parents and wondered if he'd been successful in his mission. Then she cast her gaze around the room searching for the groom. She hadn't had the privilege of seeing him yet. Ah, there he was, standing at the main entrance, looking as if he didn't have a care in the world, chatting with a bunch of his friends, a pint in his hand as usual.

A few excited gazes turned her way. She smiled at the other guests, and when she reached the bottom of the stairs, she said, "The bride looks beautiful. Not long to wait now, folks."

James caught her eye and winked at her. She walked across the black-and-white-tiled hallway and tapped Bradley on the shoulder. "Sorry to interrupt. Okay if I have a chat with you in private?"

"Of course." They stepped through the large front door into the garden. "This sounds ominous, Ruth. Is everything all right upstairs?"

Ruth waved her hand, dismissing his concerns. "Everything is fine. I told Geraldine I would check everything was going well down here. Have you checked? I wouldn't want to go around a second time if you've already done it."

Bradley's cheeks flushed, giving himself away. "I was just about to do that when Scott wanted to bend my ear about something."

She inclined her head. "A quick word? Was it important? More important than making sure your wedding goes according to plan?" *Why? Why did this man always bring out the worst in her? He was the total opposite to caring, dependable James. Lord knows what Geraldine saw in him.*

He narrowed his eyes, and his smile turned quickly into a sneer. "One day, that's all I'm asking, just give me one day off from all your snarky comments. It's obvious how much you detest me, Ruth. No idea why or what I've done to deserve that kind of hatred that I see in your eyes every time we're in the same room together. For your sake, I think it's about time you rethought your actions, don't you?"

"Is that some kind of threat, Bradley?"

His smile never reached his cold grey eyes. "Take it as it was meant, a warning. You think Geraldine doesn't notice how much you hate me? She does. Maybe you're guilty of not knowing your best friend and what she needs to ensure her happiness in this life. That task is down to me. I know what Geraldine wants, how much she craves being loved. I know every intimate part of her. Me, not *you*, so my suggestion would be for you to fall into line or move on and find yourself another best friend." He glanced at the gold watch strapped to his slender wrist. "Because in exactly ten minutes, Geraldine will be all mine."

Blood coursed through her veins, on fire. "Meaning what?"

Bradley smiled broadly and shrugged. "Simply stating a fact. Read into it what you will, Miss Private Eye."

He'd always taken the mickey out of her in the past regarding the business she'd taken over. "I'll be watching you, be aware of that. If ever you do anything out of line, I'll be on you in a flash. I don't like you. I'm usually an excellent judge of character. Maybe I've turned down my radar because of my friendship with Geraldine, but I know deep down there's a whole different side to you that has yet to come out. My advice would be for you to keep it well hidden, because if I get a whiff of it and you hurt Geraldine, I'll come down on you like a ton of bricks."

"Is that some kind of threat, Ruth?" he asked, mimicking her voice, or trying to.

"I don't have time for this, and neither do you. If you want to carry on this conversation after the wedding, you know where to find me."

"Yeah, at that two-bit office you laughingly call a detective agency. The thing is, from what I've seen of your skills, you couldn't detect a sudden drop in temperature, let alone whether someone is telling a lie or not."

"Is that the voice of experience talking? Have you lied in the past, Bradley?"

He smiled, turned his back and returned to talk to his friends again, leaving Ruth feeling livid for coming down to his level and biting back. She hadn't intended doing that, on today of all days, but the man had wound her up the wrong way. He had a habit of doing that over the years she'd known him.

She sighed and rushed towards the marquee to ensure all the preparations to do with the meal were going well. Arriving at the entrance, she gasped at the spectacle before her. Everything looked amazing, from the floral displays in the centre of the tables, to the chairs disguised in white cloth, decorated with a large lilac bow, the same colour that matched the bridesmaids' dresses. She had to admire Geraldine's taste. Her friend definitely had an exceptional skill for blending colours in order to make a substantial impact. "Is everything going well in here?"

A man in a black suit gave her the thumbs-up from the back of the tent. "We'll soon be finished, Miss. Leave it all to us."

"Glad to hear it. Not long now before they walk down the aisle." Ruth crossed the lawn and entered the house once more, ignoring Bradley as she made her way across the floor to James.

"How's Geraldine doing? Nervous, I bet?" James asked, kissing her on the cheek.

Ruth took the glass of orange juice from his hand and gulped down a large mouthful. "She's fine. Everything is going well in the marquee. We're all set to go. I'm just going to check on the band now, make sure they haven't got any last-minute hitches."

"Calm down. They seemed fine to me when I popped my head in the main room a moment ago."

"I'll go and check anyway, to put my own mind at rest. How are you both doing?" she asked Mr and Mrs Cruise.

"I'll be better when I can have a decent pint or a whisky," Mr Cruise snapped back.

"We're fine, dear. Don't worry about us," Mrs Cruise replied, patting her on the hand.

Ruth placed her hand on top of Valerie's. "Good, just enjoy the day."

"We will, dear."

Ruth handed James back his drink and left the group. She breezed into the main room, where the wedding was actually going to take place. It looked stunning and took Ruth's breath away for a second. If she thought the marquee was dressed well, it was nothing compared to what lay before her now. Even Meghan Markle would have been thrilled to have had such a display at Windsor the previous summer.

Subtle notes were coming from one side of the room. She approached the band members. "Any problems, gents?" She didn't know any of the band, they weren't local at all.

"Everything is going swimmingly here. Don't worry, Miss," the elder member of the band replied.

"Good to know." One last glance at her watch, and she returned to the hall once more. It was time to make an announcement. "Ladies and gentlemen, if I could have your attention please?" The room fell silent. "It's time for you to take up your positions in the main room before the bride makes an appearance." She gestured for the crowd to start making their way to their seats and greeted her neighbours and friends with a smile as they filtered past her and into the room.

It took seven or eight minutes for everyone to locate their seats, leaving the hallway clear, except for Bradley. He made a beeline for her. She had no place to run to, even if she wanted to avoid another confrontation with him. Instead, she beamed at him. "Well, this is it. You should be in there, awaiting your bride."

"I know where I should be, Ruth. About our conversation earlier, I meant what I said. I wanted to issue a little warning as well. If ever you try to come between me and Geraldine, you'll be the one likely to be cast adrift, not me. Got that?"

Despite seething inside, she kept her face neutral and replied, "We'll see. Enjoy your day."

He glared and marched into the room. She ensured he took up his position at the front of the room alongside his best man before she ran up the stairs to give Geraldine the all-clear.

Geraldine was standing in the bay window when she entered the room. "Are you ready for this, beautiful lady?"

The bride inhaled then exhaled several deep breaths and twisted the bouquet around in her hands a few times then looked up at her. "I don't know, am I?"

Ruth rushed across the room and grasped Geraldine by her shoulders. "It's not too late to call the whole thing off."

"Isn't it? Tell me it's just the nerves speaking and that I'm being foolish."

"It is just the nerves. As to you being foolish, no one would see it that way if you changed your mind, love."

"Bradley would have a hissing fit."

"Any doubts at all running through your mind should be listened to, Geraldine, you don't need me to tell you that."

"You do like him, don't you? Don't think I haven't noticed the look you give him at times."

Ruth placed a hand across her chest. "Me? I can't say I've noticed myself doing that. I apologise if you've spotted that in the past. You know me, I'm always thinking about work. Maybe I was distracted about something and it showed on my face. Purely coincidental, love, I promise you."

Damn, she hadn't realised she'd been that open about her dislike of the groom. She hoped against hope that Geraldine accepted her excuse. She'd hate to be the cause of her best friend refusing to walk down the aisle.

"If you say so. You would tell me if you didn't like him, wouldn't you?"

"Of course I would. I've never been one for keeping the truth hidden. If I've got anything to say, I'll say it." Ruth cupped Geraldine's chin in her hand. "Everything will be fine, you'll see. You two were made for each other." She almost choked on the final two words. What in God's name was she saying? *No, I refuse to point out that I think she'd be foolish to walk down the aisle with him. That's something she'll have to discover for herself. I have no right to interfere in someone else's marriage, whether it's just starting out or if the couple have been together a lifetime already.*

"Okay. I'd better get into position myself."

Carol coughed slightly. "You're two minutes late already."

"There you go, it's fashionable for the bride to be late. You're on course for a happy marriage. No regrets, sweetheart. Let's do this." Ruth hugged Geraldine and led her to the door.

"No regrets. There's no going back now. Thank you both for being here."

Ruth winked at her. "Don't you dare cry. Come on, smile."

Geraldine gulped. "I'm smiling on the inside. I'm struggling to transmit it to my face, though. Maybe nerves are kicking in. Let's get this over with."

Ruth walked in front of them down the grand staircase. At the bottom, she fluffed up Geraldine's dress and kissed her lightly on the cheek. "Good luck, not that you'll need it. I'm going to run ahead and take my seat. I'll instruct the band you're out here, waiting."

"You're a treasure. Thank you for being such a fabulous friend, Ruth."

Ruth strode through the main door. Geraldine's father was waiting for his daughter at the entrance. "She's coming now," she whispered in his ear. Then she nodded to the band leader to begin playing the wedding march and took her seat next to James in the front row on Geraldine's side of the church, next to her mother who anxiously reached for her hand. "Don't worry, she's fine. A little wobbly, but I think that's the norm."

"Phew, I'm glad she has you as her best friend, Ruth. You've been amazing over the years."

"Thank you, even if I did let her down about being a bridesmaid."

CHAPTER 3

THE SERVICE TURNED out to be a very special one. The bride and groom shared their own versions of the sacred vows. They were both heart-warming and gentle in nature—even Bradley pulled the stops out for that one. Which only made Ruth feel guilty for speaking to him the way she had earlier.

Merriment was prominent in what took place after the couple had tied the knot. Along with James, she was the first to congratulate the happy couple. While the bride and groom accepted further congratulations from the rest of the crowd, Ruth excused herself and left the room to ensure all was well in the marquee, ready for the reception that was about to take place.

The butler to the estate appeared beside her and said, "Looks like everything is in hand. The caterers have done an excellent job."

"I think you're right. What a relief. This is the area I was dreading going wrong the most."

The butler clicked his heels together, bowed slightly and disappeared without saying another word.

Moments later, he was leading the wedding party into the marquee, ensuring the bride and groom and all their relatives were seated at the top table first before he went back to collect the other guests.

James joined Ruth at the entrance. "I'm starving. I hope the food is up to scratch."

She chortled. "Trust you. Always thinking of your stomach. You had a large breakfast only a few hours ago."

"I know. Nerves, blame it on the nerves I've had to endure all morning. It takes a lot to organise a big event like this, you know."

A glint twinkled in his eye, and she swiped his upper arm. "Idiot. Go on, take your seat. We're on the table sitting alongside the top table."

He leaned forward and whispered, "Just think, if you'd accepted the role of bridesmaid, we'd be treated like royalty today on the top table." He ducked another swipe heading his way and ran inside before she could respond.

Everything appeared to be well organised and going swimmingly. When everyone was seated, the speeches began. Again, what Bradley had said about how he felt for Geraldine floored her, and for the second time in half an hour she wondered if she'd done him an injustice. If this was the side of Bradley her best friend had fallen in love with, then who was she to question that love?

Everyone raised their champagne glasses to the happy couple, and the meal was served. Roast beef, Yorkshire pudding and all the trimmings. It was all perfect in Ruth's eyes. She felt so proud of the way Geraldine had organised her own big day. Her gaze travelled along the top table and settled on Geraldine's father. He was hitting the drink heavily now. She couldn't help wondering where that could possibly lead to in a few hours. She also noted the jaded expression slapped on Geraldine's mother's face.

After the meal had ended, everyone was directed to go back into the main hall where the service had taken place. The room had been cleared, and the band struck up a lively tune once people began arriving. A small bar had been set up in the corner. The first person to use it was the bride's father, much to his wife's disgust.

"He's overdoing it a little," James whispered.

"Shocking behaviour. We're going to need to keep an eye on him. A lot of good your chat with the barman had in the end."

"I know, I did my best. You can't help some people though, right?"

"Yep. As long as he was soberish for when he walked Geraldine down the aisle and for the photos, I don't suppose anyone is going to begrudge him getting plastered now. I can't say it sits comfortably with me."

"Nor me. I'll keep an eye on him, don't worry."

She kissed him on the cheek. "What would I do without you?"

"We could have a frank and honest conversation about that later, if you're willing?"

Ruth grinned and rolled her eyes. "Nice try." She left him and started to circulate—knowing everyone who had been invited to the wedding had its advantages. No awkwardness because everyone knew one another. Although that brought with it certain disadvantages, too. There were a few people in the room she intended to steer clear of after falling out with them over the years. Being a private investigator made people suspicious of you all the time. That suited Ruth the majority of the time; she wasn't really the type who needed to be surrounded by friends. She was content with her life the way it was, with James and Ben.

By mid-afternoon, Ruth could tell that Geraldine was flagging. The poor girl hadn't sat down since their time in the marquee. Ruth crossed the room and stood beside Geraldine while she accepted Mrs Jordan's praise.

"I only said to Frank yesterday that I was so looking forward to this wedding. What a beautiful setting you've chosen. You're very lucky in so many ways, Geraldine. Good health and much happiness throughout your marriage. You've snagged a good one there."

"Thank you, Mrs Jordan. Did you know we're flying out on our honeymoon in a few hours?"

"I heard something on the grapevine about it being in the Caribbean. I must say, I'm a little envious. Always wanted to go there but have never had the opportunity over the years."

"Maybe your forthcoming retirement will change that."

"I doubt it. Not the state my pension pot is in, dear. Most of it got wiped out years ago. Dreadful state of affairs. That means Frank now has to continue working for another ten years or more, to make up for the loss. Bless him, he's insisted I should retire when I'm ready. After having six kids, I was ready to retire in my forties." They all laughed. "Any plans to start a family, love?"

"Gosh, I haven't really thought about that. Maybe in a year or two once we get to know each other better."

"You've got an extremely wise head on those pretty shoulders of yours, sweetie. Don't let him bully you into something you're not ready for. Having kids is a huge commitment that most people take too lightly nowadays, in my opinion." Mrs Jordan patted Geraldine on the hand then drifted off into the crowd.

"That told you," Ruth said, brushing her forehead against Geraldine's.

"Didn't it? It's been a wonderful day, but I'm feeling exhausted now. The thought of travelling to the airport and enduring that flight today is well, frankly, more than a little daunting. Why on earth did I arrange the flight so soon after the wedding?"

"I think I would have done the same thing. Once you're sitting on the plane, all this will be long behind you, you'll see. I bet you'll sleep most of the way there."

"Fingers crossed." Geraldine cast her eyes around the room.

"Looking for someone?"

"My new husband. It's been a while since I've seen him. Any idea where he's got to?"

"No. Want me to search around for him? I don't mind."

"No. He'll show up soon. He's probably nipped to the loo to empty his bladder."

"Eww…thanks, mate. Too much information. Is there anything I can do for you?"

"Not really. Actually, there is. We could change feet. Mine are worn out."

They both chuckled. Geraldine moved off to circulate the room once more. Intrigued, now the question had been raised as to where

Bradley was, Ruth went in search of him, searching room to room on the ground floor—well, in the rooms that Lady Falkirk was allowing them to use. Nothing, not a sign of him. She was just heading back to the main hallway when a man yelled. This was followed by several women screaming.

Fear filled her as she shoved past people to get to the main door. Outside, on the gravel, she found the groom. He was lying facedown on the drive, his neck twisted at an odd angle.

Her first thought was that he was already dead and there was little that could be done to revive him. Ruth glanced around her. Seeing James, she beckoned him. He rushed to be by her side. Everyone surrounding her was in a state of shock.

"Quick, give me your phone. No, on second thoughts, you ring for an ambulance. I need to find Geraldine," she said.

"What happened?"

"I don't know. Just do as I ask."

A bloodcurdling scream sounded just behind her, nearly propelling her into outer space. She turned to find Geraldine standing there, staring down at her new husband. Ruth reached for her best friend just as her legs gave way beneath her.

Ruth scanned the crowd again. *Where has James gone? I need him to help me.*

A breathless James appeared out of the blue as if she'd managed to summon him telepathically. "How did you get on?"

"The police and the ambulance are on their way."

"Good. We need to get everyone inside. They've all got to stay here, the police will need to speak to everyone. Can you do that for me, James, while I take care of Geraldine?" Ruth instructed, momentarily forgetting that James was a cop himself.

"Leave it with me. Come on, folks, let's give them some room. Please go back inside the hall, there's nothing we can do out here."

The murmuring crowd shuffled away, their gazes still transfixed on the dead body also known as the 'happy groom'.

"Are you all right, Geraldine?"

Her best friend was numb with shock, neither crying nor sobbing as expected but still, only her darting eyes moving.

"Please answer me, love. Are you all right? I need to get you inside, away from here."

She shook her head, slowly at first, and as the intensity rose, the tears finally began to fall. "What happened? Why isn't anyone helping him?"

Ruth gulped. "Because he's dead. No one could help him now. Please, come on, let me help you stand up." Ruth supported her friend by the arm and tugged her a little to get her moving. Her wedding dress was tangled around their legs, making the task a complex one. Eventually, one of the groom's mates saw them struggling through the window in the hall and came to their rescue.

"Here, let me help. Ups-a-daisy, Ger. Grab my arm, girl, and we'll have you up and inside in a jiffy."

Ruth nodded and smiled her appreciation. Without his help, she feared they would have been stuck in the same position until the police arrived. *Talking of which...I can hear sirens in the distance.* She was unsure if they belonged to the police or the ambulance at this point— that was until a car bearing a flashing blue light on its roof climbed the hill.

Ever the professional, she fished her phone out of her pocket and began snapping the scene with her camera, thinking the images would come in handy later.

The job in hand completed, she turned to watch the police car arrive, along with the crowd. Her heart sank even lower than it was already when she recognised the damn car. In it was her nemesis in the force. The one woman she detested more than walking alone through the streets on a dark night. She had a few seconds to prepare herself to deal with what lay ahead. It wasn't going to be easy. She and this policewoman had history—they disliked each other with a passion.

Crap! That's all Geraldine needs. An unemotional, uncaring detective on her case. What she really meant was a heartless detective. Maybe she should give the policewoman a chance this time round, not to let past experiences cloud her judgement before she'd even stepped out of her vehicle.

They had just managed to get Geraldine inside and deposited her with her mother and father, who had apparently sobered up pretty sharpish after what they'd witnessed, before the detective's car came to a standstill on the drive.

Ruth tried to calm her nerves by sucking in large breaths and letting them escape slowly through her scarlet lips. It didn't help one iota. Once Inspector Janice Littlejohn locked gazes with her, Ruth's heart pounded harder and faster against her ribs. No smile developed on either of their faces.

"You! What are you doing here? How did you get here before us?"

Doh! You think I wear a fancy suit for my everyday job? She swept her hands down her body, motioning towards her suit. "I'm a guest at the wedding. I would've thought that was obvious; maybe not in your case." She bit down on her tongue. *Way to go, girl. Get on the wrong side of the detective from the get-go!*

"Then you'll be better off inside with the other guests. In other words, leave us to do our job without any interference, for a change."

Ruth narrowed her gaze at the crass remark. "And what if the bride is my client?"

"I couldn't give a damn. This could be a crime scene. You'd be well advised to keep your distance if you know what's best for you. Now, if you don't mind, we have a job to do."

"Don't you want to know if anyone witnessed what happened?"

"All in good time. Go back inside, Miss Morgan. Keep out of the way of this investigation. I'll speak to you when I've dealt with the corpse."

"That *corpse* happens to be the groom."

Inspector Littlejohn's left eyebrow rose. She'd probably spent several hours at her desk, sculpting the fine line into shape instead of chasing criminals like she should have been. "The groom? Thanks for the heads-up. You're dismissed."

Dismissed? Any other inspector or cop around here would have taken me to one side to ask my opinion about the case. But not you. You're going to dig your heels in like you usually do and go about things the hard way, as usual. In the past, Ruth had solved several cases before the Inspector's investigation had seriously got off the ground. That was why the woman appeared to be permanently narked with her.

Ruth had a great rapport with most of the cops in the town. Maybe that was what ticked dear Janice off as well. Either way, Ruth knew when and where she wasn't wanted. Giving an exaggerated shrug, she left the inspector and her lacklustre sidekick, Joe Kenton, who looked suitably embarrassed by the way Littlejohn had spoken to her, and went inside as instructed.

Once inside, James quickly joined her. "My heart sank for you as soon as she turned up. Did she give you hell as usual?"

"How did you guess? She won't win. I'm going to stand at this window and watch her and her waste of space partner like a hawk. She'll mess up like she usually does. She's too damn obstinate to ask my opinion on anything, let alone a death that occurred right under my nose. You know what? It wouldn't bloomin' surprise me if at one point during the investigation she comes knocking on my door to blame me for the incident."

James gasped. "She wouldn't dare!"

"We'll see. She's an obnoxious cow, and if I can bring her down a peg or two, I will, at every opportunity. All the other cops appreciate my help in this town, bar that one. Why? Does she think I'm better than her? Maybe that's what claws at her throat the most."

"You want my take on it?" James whispered, making sure he wasn't overheard by the other guests, vying for a position at the window to observe the investigation.

She frowned. "What's that?"

"It's because she's black, and a woman, of course. A double whammy. I don't think it's personal with you two. I just reckon her job is that much tougher because of not only her gender but also because of the colour of her skin. And no, that is definitely not a racist comment."

Ruth placed her thumb and finger around her chin. Maybe James was right, for a change. Perhaps that was Littlejohn's problem, after all. "Maybe you're onto something, although I wouldn't go shouting about that down at the station if I were you. Let's just keep those thoughts between you and me, all right?"

He leaned his chin on her shoulder. "Feasible though, right?"

She turned her head and pecked him on the cheek. "Too right. Good thinking, lover boy."

Ruth watched numerous other vehicles arrive at the scene, including the ambulance and the SOCO team. The latter erected a small marquee over the body which blocked the guests' view from the hall window. This infuriated Ruth more than anything, although she hid her annoyance from the inspector, who was keenly keeping an eye on her every now and again with a sneaky glance when her head was bowed.

Did she really think Ruth couldn't see her? What an absolute amateur she was. Compared to Ruth anyway.

Finally, after a couple of hours and dozens of people complaining, the inspector began questioning the wedding guests. They were led into a room just off the main hallway where the interviews took place. No one was allowed to leave—the inspector had ordered two uniformed officers to remain at the front door to ensure that didn't happen.

After each of them was interviewed, they were given permission to leave the hall. It had been an exceptionally long day already, and now they were expected to hang around and wait to be called to give their account of what had gone on. There were over a hundred guests at this damn wedding, for goodness' sake. The thing that ticked Ruth off the most was that she knew the inspector would leave her until the end.

She watched the paramedics stretcher the groom and place him in the back of the ambulance. He was covered over with a white sheet. Ruth rushed to console Geraldine who had also witnessed the manoeuvre and was now in the process of breaking down. So far, she'd been numb to all that was going on around her. Ruth had kept half an eye on her best friend as well as watching what the inspector and her team had been up to.

Ruth sat alongside Geraldine, grasping her hand in both of hers. "It'll be all right, love, you'll see. We'll get to the bottom of what happened."

"Why would he jump like that? Take his own life when we'd only just tied the knot? Surely, if he had any doubts he was doing the wrong thing marrying me, he could have called the wedding off at any time. Was it my fault? Did I pressure him into walking down the aisle? I didn't think I had. Maybe I wasn't listening to him enough during the preparations. I thought all his negative comments were the usual things men said at times like this. If I'd known he would take his own life, I would never have organised such a big wedding. I loved him, I would've willingly eloped if that's what he'd insisted upon doing."

"Please, Geraldine, you mustn't blame yourself for this. If Bradley had issues that he wasn't willing to share with you, then that was his problem, not yours. Don't do this to yourself, I won't allow you to."

"Why leave it until the day? And why do it *after* we'd exchanged our rings? That's what I can't fathom. I'm at a loss as to what to think about this, Ruth. I need answers, and how likely is that going to be that I'll get them?"

Ruth sighed. "My guess would be highly unlikely. Let's leave it to the police, see what they can come up with."

"The police? Are they likely to find the truth? Won't you get involved in the case? I'll pay you the going rate. I have a little money set aside that was intended to be spent on the holiday. I can pay you instead."

Ruth sat back in her chair, floored by the suggestion. "You want me to find out why he would kill himself?" Geraldine nodded. "I'm not sure I'll be able to do that. If you didn't have a clue what was going on inside his head…You were the closest person to him, after all."

"I hear what you're saying, but how does a man who has every-thing, think of his life as being worthless on the day of his wedding? That's the part I don't understand." She ran a tissue under her eye, smudging her mascara even more than she had already.

"Let the detective and her team work it out for you, sweetie. I'm too close to look at this objectively."

Geraldine stared at her for a moment or two until she found her voice. "You're refusing to take me on as a client? Is that what you're saying?"

"Not outright, no. Let's bide our time on this one."

The door to the interview room opened, and DS Joe Kenton led the previous interviewee to the front door then stopped next to them. "Mrs Sinclair, if you'd like to come with me."

Geraldine frowned. "Sorry, gosh, that's me. I haven't got used to my name yet. Can Ruth come with me?"

"Why would you need someone to accompany you, Mrs Sinclair?" Kenton replied, tilting his head to one side.

"I...I don't think I can do this on my own."

"No. You can take your time, we're not in any rush. All we want is to get to the truth. If you'll follow me."

Kenton didn't even look in Ruth's direction. She didn't have the courage to speak up for what her friend wanted and plead with him to let her accompany Geraldine, because she knew she'd be slapped down in an instant.

Ruth squeezed her hand tightly before releasing it. "Good luck, love. I'll be here waiting for you." Ruth rose and helped Geraldine get to her feet. "Would it hurt for you to assist her?" she snapped when the sergeant refused to lend a hand.

"Are you able to walk by yourself, Mrs Sinclair?" he asked, scowling at Ruth.

"I think so. Maybe Ruth can come with me some of the way?"

Ruth didn't need asking twice. She held on to Geraldine's elbow and guided her towards the room, the sergeant huffing his impatience as he strode ahead of them. "Good luck again."

Geraldine's smile was a weary one. "Thank you. There's not a lot I can tell them anyway, so they're going to be disappointed. Thank you for caring and giving me a hand, Ruth."

"No problem."

Ruth stared after her friend until the door shut in her face. She was tempted to place her ear against the door to listen to the conversation but changed her mind when James waved at her to get her attention.

She walked back to him. "What's wrong?"

"How long is this going to take? One of us needs to get back to Ben. He's been cooped up in that house alone for hours. He'll think we've deserted him if we're much longer."

"You're right. The poor baby. Why don't you ring Mrs Sanders, ask her to let him out? She's still got a spare key from when we went on holiday last year."

She left James calling their old neighbour, a dear old soul who loved looking after Ben when she was called upon to tend to him, and crossed the room to where Geraldine's parents were sitting. "How are you both holding up?"

"We're surviving, Ruth. Do you think Geraldine will be able to cope in there by herself?" Valerie asked.

She hitched up a shoulder. "I don't know. I'm hoping she will."

"It's taking a bloomin' eternity. Why? You know about these things in your line of business, don't you?" Geraldine's father demanded, sounding peeved.

"It's going to take however long it takes. There are a lot of guests to speak to."

"Humph…guests who never saw a damn thing. The idiot jumped, what was there to see? Crikey, fancy doing that after you've tied the knot. Mind you, can't say the thought hasn't crossed my mind a number of times over the years."

"Ted Cruise, how dare you speak like that?"

"Wind your neck in, love. It was a figure of speech. Don't go flying off the handle."

Valerie sniffled. "You think it's been easy for me living with an alcoholic? Look at the state of you. The one day your daughter really needs your help, and you're sat here in the corner nursing another damn whisky."

Ruth wished the ground would open up and swallow her. The last thing she wanted, or needed for that matter, was to get involved in a domestic between the bride's mother and father. She had no words for either of them—correct that, she could think of a hatful she could direct at Mr Cruise but knew if she did that, she would lose Geraldine's friendship in a second. No, she would have to bite on the inside of her mouth until the argument died down.

"Has it ever occurred to you why I drink, woman? Well, has it?" Mr Cruise slurred.

"It doesn't take much for a man to turn to the bottle. How dare you blame your inability to curb such urges on me? How very dare you?"

Mr Cruise closed his eyes and tilted his head from side to side as he mimicked his wife's words, obviously thinking she was in the throes of nagging him.

Ruth looked on in amazement, her mind whirring. *If this is married life years down the line after a wedding takes place, then I'll definitely be staying single in the foreseeable future.*

"That's what you women do, drive your men to drink with your nagging. I've had my share of it over the years. After the honeymoon period is over, that's when you women think you can control us."

"Really? Well, if that's what you think, I'll be knocking on my solicitor's door first thing in the morning."

"Ha! It's Sunday tomorrow, you daft mare."

"Please, Mr and Mrs Cruise, falling out like this isn't helping. Won't you both calm down and consider what your daughter is going through? She'll be relying on you over the coming weeks or months to help her through this."

Valerie faced her husband and nodded. "Ruth is right, dear. We should stop all this pointless bickering and think of what's best for Geraldine. I'm aware it's only the drink talking."

"It is not. All it does is make me think straight. I'm trapped. If you want a divorce, I'll give you one without a moment's hesitation."

Ruth sighed and rolled her eyes, glancing over her shoulder to see if she could urge James to rescue her. He was busy chatting to a few stragglers who'd already been interviewed and hadn't as yet taken the hint from the police to go home.

"Please, Mr and Mrs Cruise, can we not do this, today of all days? What about putting Geraldine first? She's going to need your support to get through this. Her husband has just died. She'll need you to help with the arrangements for his funeral."

Geraldine's parents had the decency to look embarrassed.

"Ruth's right, Ted. We should stop squabbling and put our daughter first. Shall we call a temporary truce?"

Ted Cruise glared at his wife and then offered a reluctant nod. "Deal. But this conversation will be revisited in a week or so, I can guarantee you that, Valerie. Something has to change. I can't stand things as they are."

Valerie closed her eyes and nodded. When she opened them again, Ruth could tell she was trying hard to hold back the tears threatening to fall. Before she had a chance to whip Valerie away from her alcoholic husband, the door to the room the police were using to interview people opened, and a shocked-looking Geraldine emerged in a daze.

Ruth rushed across the room and flung an arm around Geraldine's shoulders. "Are you all right? You look in shock, lovely. Anything I can do?"

"Get me to a chair."

"Of course." Ruth guided Geraldine to the edge of the room, close to the door, and helped her into a vacant chair. She sat beside her, gathering her hands in her own. Her best friend's hands were freezing, despite the temperature being in the high twenties. Ruth rubbed at them, trying to transfer some of her warmth. "What's wrong, Geraldine? You have to tell me." The door to the interview room opened again, and DS Kenton walked towards her. "What have you said to her? I demand to know."

"Nothing. We simply asked a few questions pertinent to the case. If you'd care to join us, Miss Morgan."

"What? Now? You'll have to wait until I make sure my friend is all right."

"Someone else can sit with her. Aren't they her parents?" He pointed over to where Geraldine's warring parents were sitting.

"Yes, but they're indisposed at the moment." Ruth frantically turned to search for James. "James, can you do me a favour and sit with Geraldine? They want to see me." James hurried across the room to be with her and sat in the seat next to Geraldine. "I won't be long, and then we'll get you out of here, Geraldine."

"Yes, I want to go home. I need to go home," Geraldine pleaded, her voice catching on a sob.

"When you're ready," the young DS prompted.

Walking towards the room, mixed emotions filled Ruth. She was struggling to keep her anger in check after the way Geraldine had left the room, but she knew it was imperative that she do just that. She'd never liked coming face to face with the inspector before. There was just something about her attitude that rubbed her up the wrong way. *Calm down, try and keep her onside. I need to do that for Geraldine's sake.*

Inspector Littlejohn was sitting erect behind a desk. Kenton shut the door and took his position standing alongside her. "Sit down, Miss Morgan," the inspector ordered.

"Will this take long? Only I'd like to take care of Geraldine. Whatever you said to her has obviously had a profound effect on her."

"It will take as long as necessary. The quicker you answer the questions, then the quicker you can get back to your friend."

Ruth sat, remaining on the edge of her seat, her hands in her lap and her thoughts still with Geraldine. "Fire away."

"Did you see Mr Sinclair before his death?"

"What kind of question is that? Of course I saw him, this was his wedding day. He married my best friend, in case you're unaware."

"I'm aware. I meant just before his death. I'm fully aware of what day it is."

"He was mingling with his guests. I might have spotted him here and there."

"How long have you known him?"

"About five years all told."

The inspector nodded and wrote something down in her notebook. "Did you get on with him?"

"Why? Where is this leading?"

"Answer the question, Miss Morgan," Kenton said, his tone harsh, as if he were speaking to an unruly drunk after kicking out time.

"Of course I got on with him, he was Geraldine's boyfriend, erm...husband."

"When was the last time you saw him?"

"Are you serious? What type of question is that in the circumstances?"

"I'd call it a pertinent one, Miss Morgan," Littlejohn insisted, her tone clipped.

Ruth let out an exasperated breath. "Moments before you arrived. He was facedown on the gravel, his neck broken by the look of it."

"Why do you always have to be so acerbic?"

"I don't know, why do you think?" It hadn't taken them long to enter into their usual battle of wills.

"This is getting us nowhere. Either you answer my questions properly, and without any further sarcasm on your part, or we'll take you back to the station to conduct our enquiries."

That's told me. Okay, we'll do things your way for now, Janice.

"I want to know what you said to upset Geraldine so much."

"We merely asked her some questions about her husband. Oh, we also might have told her that we were treating this enquiry as a murder investigation, too."

Ruth's tired eyes flew open. "Murder enquiry? On what grounds?"

"On the grounds that, contrary to what all you guests believe about the man's death, we believe he was pushed."

"What? How can you even say that?"

"We have our reasons behind thinking along those lines. Now, shall we start this interview again from the top?"

"You can try. My answers won't alter from the ones I've given you already. Murdered? Who'd have thunk it?"

"Who indeed? Again, I'm asking you to cast your mind back a little. After the wedding, did you see the groom, before he fell to his death?" the inspector added quickly, anticipating that Ruth would pounce on her wayward wording again.

"No. Everyone was busy milling around after we'd eaten. The last time I saw him was when he was raising a toast to his new wife in the marquee."

"What time was that?"

Ruth puffed out her cheeks, contemplating her answer. "Around an hour before his death, I suppose. I can't give you a specific time because, in my book, it would be rude to stand at a wedding checking my watch every few seconds. I'm sure you'd feel the same, right?"

"Okay, I'll give you that one. Did you notice Mr Sinclair having words with anyone?"

Ruth's shoulders hunched forward. "You're going to think I'm being sarcastic when I say this, but I'm truly not; he 'had words' with a lot of people, it was his wedding. He circulated the room just like Geraldine did."

"I'm glad you raised your friend's name. Do you think she had any reason to kill off her husband?"

Gobsmacked by the inspector's ridiculous suggestion, she shook her head vehemently. "What a dumb question. Why on earth would she go through all the trouble and expense of organising a wedding, her wedding, if her intention was to kill him directly after the ceremony had taken place? What about the honeymoon?"

"What about it?"

"Have you checked if they were both booked on the flight? Surely if you had you wouldn't be asking such inane questions."

"We've yet to look into the ins and outs of everything. As I said, we're simply asking questions that we feel are pertinent to our enquiry at this stage. Now, can you think of a reason why Geraldine would want to kill her husband?"

"No, not in the slightest. Not in a million, trillion years—does that emphasise my point enough?"

"A little excessively I'd say. All right then, can you think of anyone attending the reception who could do this to Mr Sinclair?"

"No. Not that I go around trying to read people's minds. I'm still at a loss to know how you think he was pushed to his death and didn't merely fall."

"This is getting us nowhere. I thought you of all people would be willing to help us with our enquiries. I suppose I was wrong about that. Understandable, given what's gone on in the past between us."

"That has nothing, nothing to do with this. If Bradley was murdered, and that's a big *if*, then of course I would want to know who did it and why. If only for Geraldine's sake. Look at it from her point of view. She's spent the last five years planning this wedding. At the last minute, her father pulled the plug on the funding side of things and she's ended up footing the bill herself. Do you seriously think after going through all that effort, that at the first opportunity presented to her, she would push her husband off the turret? That's absolutely absurd."

"Is it? Maybe that's what a lot of people would think. Maybe this was her way of shifting the blame from herself."

Ruth shook her head slowly. "You're sick if you believe that."

"Stranger things have happened."

"I think you're not only barking up the wrong tree but you're in the totally wrong forest. Okay, think about this for a moment if you will. If a wife is going to bump off her husband, wouldn't she at least have bothered to have insured him first? Otherwise, what would be her motive for killing him right after they had exchanged vows?"

Kenton glanced at the inspector, and she turned to face the sergeant, chewing on her bottom lip as if Ruth's words had sunk in and set her mind racing.

"You might have a valid point. If she didn't do it, then who else could have killed him?"

"That, my dear inspector, is your job to find out."

"What about her parents?"

Ruth shrugged. "What about them?"

"Do you think either of them are likely to have pushed him?"

"No, again, what would their motive be?"

"We'll see. They're the next two people I want to interview."

"Crap, do you have to do that today?"

The inspector's head tilted a little. "Is there a specific reason why you think I should delay that?"

"For a start, I believe Mr Cruise is slightly inebriated, so you won't get much sense out of him, and secondly, I believe Mrs Cruise has been traumatised enough by today's events."

"By the wedding?"

"No, not as such. I recently overheard her telling Mr Cruise that she intends seeking a divorce."

"On her daughter's wedding day?"

"Apparently, weddings can bring out the worst in people, if the groom being killed is anything to go by."

"So, who do you think is guilty of pushing him?"

Ruth cradled her chin between her finger and thumb. "Again, I can't for the life of me think of anyone who would want to kill him. Is there anything else? Only I'd like to get back to Geraldine. The shock must be traumatic for her."

"You're dismissed on the proviso that we can drop in at any time to question you further."

"Of course."

Ruth started to stand and stopped midway when the inspector added, "Oh, and I'd ask you to keep your distance on this one. Any interference on your part, and I'll have no hesitation in banging you up in a cell."

"For what? The last I heard, we were living in a free country. Has that changed recently? If so, I was unaware any new laws had come into force."

The inspector shook her head, her anger glinting in her dark-brown eyes. Kenton stepped around the desk and showed Ruth out of the room without the inspector uttering another word. Ruth couldn't help doing an imaginary strike in the air in her mind. *Idiot. When will she learn to be a proper detective and detect things rather than spending most of her time clutching at straws?*

Geraldine was still being comforted by James when she left the room. "Hello, you. How are you feeling?"

"Did they tell you?"

Ruth nodded.

James frowned. "Tell you what? What am I missing here?"

She turned to look over her shoulder. Then, once she saw that Kenton wasn't standing behind her listening to their conversation, she told him, "The police reckon that Bradley was pushed."

James let out a long whistle. "No way. Who would do such a thing? On his bloody wedding day as well?"

She pleaded with her eyes for him to lower his voice so the other people in the room didn't hear.

"I don't know, but I'm going to find out," Ruth replied, thrusting her shoulders back with determination.

"Would you, Ruth, please, for me?" Geraldine beseeched her.

Placing her hands onto Geraldine's, she nodded. "And it won't cost you a penny. This one is on me, love. We'll get to the bottom of this, I promise you."

Now, if only I can get up to the turret to have a look around.

CHAPTER 4

RUTH WAS DISAPPOINTEDLY TURNED AWAY from the turret by the officer on guard. Not long after, she suggested to James that they should take Geraldine back to their house with them.

"I'm fine. Please don't fuss. I'll go back home with Mum and Dad. I don't want to put you two to any bother."

"Are you sure?" Ruth asked, unsure how her friend was going to cope once she was back at the house, the home she'd shared with Bradley for the past five years.

"I'm sure. Don't worry about me. I could do with some time alone to go over things in my mind. I'm exhausted with all the planning I've had to do with the wedding and now, in the next few days, I'll have a funeral to arrange."

"Look, love, you don't have to go through this alone. James and I will help where we can."

Geraldine smiled wearily. "No, I need you to concentrate on finding the person responsible for killing him, Ruth. Please, that has to be your priority. Promise me you won't let me down on that front?"

"I promise. If you're sure? If you change your mind, just call us. I'll ring you later, make sure you're all right."

"Please, can you leave it for the rest of the day? I don't even want to see Mum and Dad, but they're staying with me; it's going to be hard shutting them out. It's something I need to do, though. I need peace and quiet to reflect. It's been such a whirlwind of a day. A new bride one minute and a widow the next. How could you ever explain that to a stranger? I'm tired, I just want to curl up like a cat on my bed. I'll probably bawl my eyes out once I'm at home. I refuse to do it here, in front of those left behind. I don't care if they think of me as a hard cow."

"No one would dare think of you as that, love. Everyone grieves differently. Don't you worry about what other people might think, you just do what's right for you, you hear me?"

"Thank you, Ruth. I'm such a lucky girl to have someone as dear as you as my closest friend."

"Nonsense. I'd never let you down at such a heartbreaking time. Will you ring me if you need to chat? Day or night, it makes no odds to me."

"I will. Thank you for everything you've done so far. I meant what I said about paying you. I need to know what happened and why someone felt they had to take Bradley's life, today of all days."

"We'll see. I mean, yes, I'm willing to help you to find out that information. What I meant to say was that I don't want to be paid for it. Think of it as a gift from me."

"I wouldn't expect you to do it for no money at all. We'll chat about this more once I've had a rest and tried to put things into perspective." Fresh tears welled up.

Ruth reached for her and grasped her in a loving hug. "You'll be fine. I promise you I will get to the bottom of this."

Sniffling, Geraldine pulled away and nodded. "Thank you. I'd better see if the police have finished with Mum and Dad now, or maybe I should go home alone. What do you think?"

Ruth glanced over her shoulder to see only Mrs Cruise sitting there. "I can run you home. I think your father is still being interviewed."

"You're a treasure. Thank you."

Ruth went in search of James to tell him she was leaving. He said he had a few more people to say cheerio to before he could leave and that he would see her back at the house.

The journey into town was full of sighs and a comfortable silence between them. Ruth had said everything that needed to be said. Geraldine was aware that their friendship would enter new territory going forward, during the search for the truth.

When she drew up outside the home Geraldine and Bradley had shared together, Geraldine hesitated until Ruth patted her on the leg and told her she'd accompany her inside. Ruth opened the front door with her friend's key. Geraldine halted for a split second in the doorway and then turned to her.

"I can smell his aftershave. Do you think it's a sign, or am I being silly?"

Ruth shrugged. "I don't think you're being silly in the slightest. I've heard this sort of thing happening before, not that I've been a great believer in the past."

"Can't you smell it?" She circled a spot in front of her, urging Ruth to inhale a lungful of air from that very spot.

Ruth did just that but smelt nothing. She shook her head. "Sorry. I've usually got a good nose, but there's nothing there for me."

Geraldine gasped. "You don't think it's his spirit, do you?" she whispered, her eyes widening as she spoke.

"Maybe. Let's not worry about that now. Let's get you inside and out of that dress."

"I'm fine. I appreciate the lift, Ruth. You can leave me alone now."

Despite having doubts, Ruth did as she was asked and left the house after giving her friend a final reassuring hug.

Her mind whirled frantically during the couple of minutes' drive back to her beautiful cottage. Where would the investigation begin? She wasn't privy to the notes the inspector had taken from the guests. No one she'd spoken to at the reception knew anything about Bradley's movements immediately before he'd plunged to his death. Where the heck did she go for answers? She feared this investigation would turn out to be her toughest one to date, in more ways than one, what with very few clues to go on, plus she'd be under the added stress of having to solve the case because the victim had been married to her best friend.

Feeling as if her world was closing in on her, she poured herself a glass of wine and took it outside to play ball with Ben. She pulled out a chair on the patio and sat, staring at her glass, unaware of Ben dropping the ball at her feet until he pawed her leg and whimpered. "Sorry, boy. Here, go fetch."

Her devoted companion happily ran back and forth dozens of times until exhaustion took over and he flopped down beside her.

James came out of the back door moments later. He kissed her forehead and placed his can of beer on the table. "What a day, eh, love? No one could have predicted it would have ended this way."

"Too right. I want to support Geraldine all I can, you know I do, but I've been sitting here pondering how the heck I'm going to do that. Where do I even begin?"

James, who was a constable at the local police station, shook his head. "I think you're too close to this one. Why don't you give it a miss and let Inspector Littlejohn deal with it?"

"For one thing, I've promised Geraldine after her pleading with me to take the case on, and for another, I can't have Janice Littlejohn getting one over on me."

"You're an idiot at times. Adorable, but still an idiot. She's going to have information to hand that will be valuable in solving the case. I'll never understand why you two don't get along."

"Because she's a pain in the rear. Has been from the first time I met her."

"That's a bit harsh. I think you're exaggerating a touch there."

"Maybe just a soupçon. It's true in most cases, though. I've usually got a suspect in mind within a few days because I'm tenacious and determined. She's just downright obnoxious. No one ever wants to confide in her, so she has to do things the hard way."

"That's exactly my point. The reason people in this town open up to you is because you've lived here all your life. She's been here, what? Three years, if that?"

"And that's my problem, how?"

He sighed. "All I'm saying is, that the townsfolk are more likely to open up to you than they are to a complete stranger. Anyway, her reputation down at the station is a pretty good one. She's impressed a lot of people in her time on the force."

"Doing what? No, don't answer that. I don't want to know whose bedpost she's put a notch in since her arrival." Ruth shuddered at the image she'd managed to conjure up.

"Now you're just being plain ridiculous. As far as I can tell, she works hard and always has since she joined, often being overlooked when promotions have been handed out."

"There, that's probably why she's such a spiky character then."

"Whatever. I'm going to fix myself a bacon sandwich. Do you want one?"

"You only ate a few hours ago. Do you have worms?"

"No. My energy is sapping because of what we've had to contend with up there. I didn't think the dinner was up to much anyway, did you?"

"It was all right. Can't say it will ever be a memorable wedding in that respect."

He leaned forward as he stood, his face inches from hers. "No one can make a roast dinner like my sweetheart."

Her anxiety leaked away. "You're such a charmer. Don't think I don't know what you're up to. You say the nicest things when you want to keep me onside."

"And you wonder why I don't dish out compliments that often."

"Maybe it's a case of me not being used to you dishing out compliments."

"What utter tripe, and you know it." He stormed off in a huff, but when he got to the door, he looked back and winked.

He was a good man. They were terrific together. Rarely ever fell out, which begged the question: why hadn't she walked down the aisle with him yet? She was aware men like James were few and far between, especially nowadays when most men thought with the dangly bit between their legs. He was different. She just wasn't ready to take the plunge and go the whole hog yet. He understood—at least she thought he did.

A sudden thought jumped into her mind. Her mother and father were on holiday. They had been gutted to miss the wedding, but they'd had another appointment they couldn't get out of down in Cornwall and had decided to combine the trip with a few weeks travelling around the county in their campervan. Her mother would have her guts for garters if she didn't ring her to tell her how the wedding had gone. She rushed inside and picked up the house phone and dialled her mother's mobile number.

"Hello, Ruth. We were just talking about you. Are you having a wonderful time at the wedding? I bet Geraldine's dress is a stunner. She has such an eye for fashion that girl, you could learn a lot from her."

"Gee, thanks, Mum. I have something to tell you. Are you sitting down?"

"Oh my. Whatever is the matter? Wait a minute...are you at home? You sound so serious. Come on, tell me. I'm sitting down now. Has something happened to James? He hasn't ditched you after all this time, has he? You know what raw emotions a wedding brings to the surface..."

"Mum, if you'll take a breath and listen for a second, I'll fill you in. And no, this has nothing to do with James, we're as solid as granite."

"Then what is it?"

"I'm sorry to have to break this to you while you're away but"—her mother's gasp filled the line between them—"although the wedding took place as planned, afterwards tragedy struck."

"What do you mean? What kind of tragedy? Oh no, Geraldine's father didn't have a stroke, did he?"

"No, Mum. Stop jumping to conclusions and listen."

"I'm listening. Get on with it, then, child." Her mother's tone was full of scolding.

"After the wedding and the reception took place, sadly, the groom, Bradley, passed away."

Her mother screamed. Ruth was too late in holding the phone

away from her and shook her head when her inner ear rang uncomfortably.

"You could have warned me you were going to do that, Mum. You nearly deafened me."

"Nonsense. It would take more than a little squeal from me to do that."

Ruth might have known her mother, an ex-doctor, would come back with a sharp retort along those lines.

"How did he pass away? Was it because of the stress?"

"No. Unfortunately the police think he was murdered." Ruth held the phone away from her ear as a precaution this time. Good job, too, as her mother did indeed let out another high-pitched scream.

When she'd calmed down, her voice appeared a little strained. "Murdered? How?"

"Seems someone pushed him from the turret at Carmel Cove Hall. I was one of the first to attend the scene. His neck was broken. Mum, it was awful." She didn't know why she had trouble holding back the tears.

"There, there, dear. Oh my, it must have been awful for you. Poor Geraldine, newly married and already a widow. Whatever will she do now?"

"I'll offer her as much support as she needs, Mum. I won't leave her high and dry. It's devastating to think the happiest day of her life has turned into one of the saddest a few hours later."

"Will you be investigating the crime for her?"

"That's the plan. I tried to get up to the turret, but the police blocked my path. That Inspector Littlejohn is in charge of the case. You know how much we rub each other up the wrong way."

"I do. Maybe you should have a word with her, impress upon her how important it is that Geraldine receives the answers to her questions quickly."

"Fat chance of that happening, Mum, she's always treated me as a second-class citizen. I reckon she's going to dig her heels in more on this investigation because I'm personally involved with the victim's family."

"You think so? Are you sure about that?"

"That's my perception. She questioned me at the reception and then warned me to stay out of her way. The trouble is, Geraldine has said that she wants to employ me to find out how Bradley died. I've said I would and that I wouldn't charge her a fee, but I'm not sure how I'm going to find out what I need to know with that woman on the damn case. I'm between a rock and a hard place on this one."

"Hush now. You'll figure it all out. I have faith in you, your father has, too. He sends his love by the way. We're parked up by a beautiful lake at the moment, and he's out there feeding the ducks with some leftover bread we had from yesterday. We've been buying fresh bread daily and fresh cream cakes. I fear I'm going to be the size of our bungalow when I get back."

Her mother infuriated her at times. She'd always been a slender size eight to ten but had been on a constant diet throughout her whole life. "Mum, you're on holiday. Enjoy yourself and the food you eat and worry about the consequences when you get home."

"I will. Sorry, I branched off the subject. Do you want us to come home? We don't mind in the slightest."

"Honestly, there's nothing you can do around here anyway. The investigation will have to run its course. You stay there and have some fun."

"I'm going to be riddled with guilt if I do that, dear. What about the funeral? We should come home for that."

"No idea when that is likely to be held as yet. The man died barely a few hours ago. I suppose we're not likely to know when the funeral will take place until the PM has been carried out. They won't release his body until then."

"I suppose you're right. Give us a ring when you hear anything else. We'll drop everything and come back to show our respects. Thank heavens his mother and father aren't still alive. No doubt they'll be turning in their graves until his murder is solved. You will do your best for them, won't you, dear? I know you haven't had the best of relationships with Bradley in the past, but you'll be able to overcome any prejudices you had against the man, yes?"

"We've had a few heated arguments and disagreements in the past, Mum, that's all. Nothing that I would class as major. Hey, there wasn't anything underlying in that statement, was there?"

"I don't have a clue what you're talking about. Would you care to enlighten me?"

"You know damn well what I'm saying. I would never—I *could* never—cause another human being harm in that way. To think that you'd have the affront to suggest such a thing abhors me, quite frankly."

"Now wait just a minute. I did not—and I would *never*—suggest such a thing. Climb down off your high horse, young lady, and think about what you've just accused me of."

Ruth cringed. She was feeling sensitive for a number of reasons right now and had dropped her guard to her mother. "Sorry. Let's forget either of us said anything."

"Very well, but I wasn't casting aspersions, I promise you. I'm hurt that you should think that of me."

"I've already apologised, Mum. It's been a very long day, and it isn't over yet. I'm going to hang up now before either of us says something else we might regret. Enjoy the rest of your holiday and send my love to Dad."

"I will. Ruth, before you go, I might not say this that often, but I do love you, dear. More than you've given me credit for over the years."

"I know, Mum. I love you, too."

Ruth replaced the phone in its docking station and looked up to see James leaning against the doorframe stuffing his face with a bacon sandwich, ketchup oozing out the side and running down his chin. She laughed. "I'd suggest grabbing a serviette out of the drawer."

"Oops, I do it every time." He went back into the kitchen and called out, "Are you all right?"

"Yes. Just mum being mum. Saying one thing and meaning another. One of these days, she'll think before she opens her mouth."

"What did she say?" He reappeared in the doorway and tilted his head then took another bite of his doorstep of a sandwich, which consisted of equal quantities of bread and bacon from what she could see.

"Nothing, it's not worth discussing. I'm going upstairs to get out of my suit, then I think I'll take Ben out for a walk to clear my head."

He gulped down the mouthful he was chewing and with puppy-dog eyes said, "Do you want me to join you? I could do with blowing the cobwebs out of my head with a stroll along the coastal path. We haven't ventured up there together in a while."

Ruth nodded. "That would be lovely. Give me ten minutes."

"That'll give me time to finish this off and get changed myself."

FIFTEEN MINUTES LATER, they set off in the car along with the super excited Ben who constantly paced the back seat, as far as his safety harness would allow anyway.

They reached the car park, paid the fee and began their brisk walk across the hill and along the coastal path. In total, the path ran along the rugged clifftops for five miles. The route was circular in nature, coming back across the various fields that took them away from the breathtaking views that were always accompanied by a sea breeze, no matter how fine the weather was. It was an ideal evening for stretching one's legs after the trauma of the day. Neither of them spoke about what had taken place earlier. Instead, they focused on keeping Ben away from the edge, having to put him back on his lead at certain points where the path was narrow and had a severe drop into the sea; however, most of the time he was off-leash, content to stick close beside them. It was a different matter entirely once the route diverted into the fields. There, the little rascal took off once he picked up the scent of a bunny Ruth and James had spotted in the distance.

"His nose never fails him," Ruth said, smiling at her adorable dog's antics.

"He's a little tyke when he puts his mind to it. Stubborn as a mule when you call him back, too, once he's picked up a scent."

"They always manage to outrun him, though. Dread to think what he might do to one if he ever came face to face with it."

"My guess is that he'd run a mile. I think most dogs would. It's nice to get out together. We should do this more often. We both work too damn hard, especially you."

"It's hard. I'm still trying to build the business. It could take years to get established. You knew that when I first set it up."

He stopped and reached for her, placing her hands in his. "Don't get me wrong, I wasn't complaining. You have a right to run your own business the way you see fit, Ruth, even if it does encroach on the time we should be spending together."

"I'm sorry. I didn't mean to jump, if that's the way it came across. I don't know what's got into me today."

"Seeing a dead body, the corpse of your best friend's husband, would be the likely cause of that, love. I understand you're feeling fragile at the moment. You'll get over it. So will Geraldine, eventually."

She squeezed his hands. "I hope she will. I'm not sure I would if anything like that ever happened to you. I'd be devastated beyond words."

They shared a long kiss, and then he pushed her away from him. "I'm not going anywhere. I promise you'll never be put in that position."

"Glad to hear it. I'd be lost without you by my side or sharing my bed with me at night."

CHAPTER 5

RUTH WOKE up the following day when the warmth of the sun slipped through the curtains and touched her face. She stretched—the bed next to her was empty. James was on earlies that week, starting work at six. A sudden feeling of desertion washed over her. She knew she was being silly because he'd be back at three-thirty that afternoon. She stretched the knots out of her body and reprimanded herself. *At least James will be home later, unlike Bradley.*

Throwing back the quilt, she hoisted herself out of her warm bed and padded barefoot across the carpet and into the compact but beautiful en suite they'd paid to have installed the previous year. She was tempted to run and luxuriate for a while in the claw-footed bath she had sourced. An expert in town had touched up the enamel. She decided against having a soak. Her priority was to visit Geraldine, see what sort of night she'd had.

She opted to take a quick shower in the main bathroom instead and had dried her long red hair and slipped on a pair of jeans and a T-shirt within minutes. Ben must have heard her walking around because he appeared in the doorway, panting eagerly to be let out into the garden or more likely to be taken on a long walk down by the river.

Ruth patted her thighs to beckon him. "Come here, boy."

He bounded across the six feet between them in seconds and rubbed his head against her leg. She kissed him above the eye. He moaned loudly, the way he always did when she openly showed him any form of affection.

"I'll have to delay our walk this morning, boy. I need to go and check on Geraldine first. You understand, don't you?"

He sat in front of her and twisted his head from side to side as she spoke then gave her his paw.

"You're a sweetheart. I'll make it up to you later, I promise."

She ventured downstairs and dropped a piece of granary bread in the toaster and filled the kettle. While she waited for it to boil, she opened the three envelopes she'd picked up from the doormat on her way into the kitchen. The first was a reminder that her car tax was due. The second, a letter seeking a donation for breast cancer that she put aside to make a worthwhile contribution later when she had more time. And the final letter was a handwritten thank-you message from one of her clients. She read the note with a smile pulling at her lips. The woman had literally taken her cheating husband to the cleaners. He was a successful businessman in Bristol and had been cheating on her for years. Thanks to Ruth's tenacious digging, she'd found out that he'd not only had numerous affairs with a bagful of women but even had a woman tucked up in a flat who he was 'servicing' a couple of times a week. The outcome had seen the couple in the divorce courts —her investigation notes had proven pivotal in achieving what the wife needed to bring up their two young kids. The female judge had shown the husband nothing but contempt, and she'd ensured the woman had full time use of the family home, which was a huge mansion in the sticks, until the children were eighteen and had left school. The rest of their funds and possessions were split fifty-fifty, much to the husband's disgust. He'd shouted in response, sarcastically urging the judge to consider taking the shirt off his back as well.

Ruth had been in court that day, and her eagle eye had detected that the judge found his tone offensive during the case and, upon hearing his outlandish remark, was sorely tempted to arrest him for contempt of court. How she had refrained from doing that Ruth would never know. She and her client had cheered and hugged each other in the courtroom under the hateful gaze of the husband, soon to be the ex-husband. The icing on the cake was that when he'd had all his assets stripped from him, even the girl, whom he had tucked up warmly in a flat, didn't want to know about her 'sugar daddy'. The last Ruth heard was that all the man could afford, after the sentence was passed, was a crummy bedsit in the heart of Bristol, after the judge had awarded the wife an exorbitant amount of maintenance for their two children. Karma, she was a wonderful ally at times.

Ruth smiled and slid the thank-you note into a folder she kept, to do with her business, in the bookcase in the kitchen. The toast popped up as the kettle finished boiling. After slathering the toast in marmalade, she sat at the table to enjoy her breakfast before she set off.

The ever-hopeful Ben sat at her feet just in case she dropped a morsel his way. She didn't. After visiting the vet's the week before, she'd put him on a diet. He didn't look chunky, but since he'd been castrated, he'd put on an astonishing ten kilos. She was determined to shift at least five of those over the next few months by cutting back on his meals and upping his exercise regime. Oh, and possibly knocking his treats on the head, although she thought that would be their toughest challenge of all. Ben loved his treats.

"Come on, you little monkey, it's time for us to make a move." She locked up the house, secured Ben in the back seat, placing his harness in the seat belt holder, and drove to Geraldine's house. She parked behind an old Ford, likely twenty years old, and walked up the small front path to the semi-detached house Geraldine had shared with Bradley. Ruth poised ready to ring the bell but was distracted when she heard raised voices coming from the rear of the property. Dipping down the side access, she entered the back garden to find out what all the fuss was about.

She found Mr and Mrs Cruise going at it, hammer and tongs. Mrs Cruise was in the process of hitting her husband with an umbrella of all things, until Ruth charged in and snatched the weapon out of her hand.

"What in God's name do you think you're doing? You two should be ashamed of yourselves, behaving like this when your daughter needs you the most." The couple had the decency to look mortified by their over-the-top actions. "Where's Geraldine?"

The husband and wife stared at her, and Mrs Cruise shrugged. "She went out about an hour ago and hasn't returned yet."

"What? And you sat back and let her take off like that? What were you thinking? What frame of mind is she in today?"

Mrs Cruise looked down at her slippered feet. "I'm sorry. We're sorry. She was very quiet. Oh, gosh, what have we done, Ted?"

Her husband swept Ruth aside to comfort his sobbing wife.

"I don't have time for your shenanigans. Any idea where she went? Has she taken her mobile?"

"She mentioned something about going for a walk on the coast. I didn't think anything of it. Thought the fresh air would do her some good and no, her mobile is on the dining room table."

Ruth let out an exasperated breath. "I'll try and find her. I suggest you figure out what you both need to do with regard to your relationship before Geraldine returns. It's your support she'll be craving now, not your damn bickering like teenagers."

Mr Cruise opened his mouth to offer a rebuttal.

Ruth silenced him with a raised hand. "I don't want to hear it. Your daughter is my priority right now, and you know what? She should be yours, too."

Ruth tore out of the garden and ran back to the car. She floored the accelerator and drove up the hill towards the coastal path she and James had taken with Ben the previous evening. Something in her gut was urging her to get there quickly.

Ben paced the back seat, sensing something wrong. He started whimpering when their destination became clear. They had come here regularly since he was a pup in arms. "Bear with me, mate. I have to find Geraldine, and quickly." She parked in the gravelled area, scrabbled around in the console for an odd pound coin and stuck the parking ticket on the windscreen. Then she unfastened the clasp confining Ben and slipped the leash around his neck. "Promise me you'll behave. We need to find Geraldine before we can go on a proper walk, lovely."

Ben licked the side of her face as if he understood what she'd said.

After locking the car, she and Ben raced towards the clifftop. There was a mist shrouding the coastal path up ahead, which was common at this hour of the morning most days, before the sun shifted position and its rays fully hit the top of the cliffs. She had no idea which way Geraldine had gone, or indeed if she had even come up here. She'd noticed Geraldine's car was still outside the house when she'd left. That didn't mean anything, though. Her friend could have easily flagged down a cab to bring her up here.

She cupped her hands around her mouth and shouted, "Geraldine, are you here?"

There was no response other than the sound of the waves crashing against the rocks beneath her. Fear wrapped itself around her heart. She'd never felt as alone as she did in that instant. Where was James when she needed him?

"Come on, Ben. We need to up our pace, boy." With every step she took along the narrow path, Ben on the leash close to her side, her heart beat louder and harder, mimicking a bass drum as it rose to a crescendo like in one of the old black-and-white movies. She rounded the crest of the hill that dipped down the other side and shouted again. "Geraldine. If you're here, please answer me." This time, above the sound of the wild sea below her, she heard a faint call, or thought she did. Ben stopped and whimpered, his nose to the ground. He peered over the edge of the path. Ruth yanked back on his leash. "Come away, Ben. What is it, boy? Geraldine? Is that you?"

Again, a weak voice responded. She could just make out her name being called.

"Geraldine. Where are you, love?" Although she'd asked the question, she had an inkling she knew the answer. Ben had already signified that her friend was possibly in danger.

"Please, Ruth, get help. I can't hold on much longer."

Ruth inched herself closer to the edge, at the same time restraining Ben by wrapping his leash around her hand several times. He barked as she lost her footing when a few of the smaller rocks shifted beneath her feet and tumbled over the edge.

"Damn, if we're not careful we'll be joining her. I need to get help, boy. Let's back up." She fished her phone out of her pocket and dialled the emergency services. "I'm sorry to trouble you. Please, I don't know which service I need."

"Calm down, madam. Just tell me what's happened," the male voice replied.

"I'm up on the coastal path above Carmel Cove. My friend, she's hanging on to the cliff. I think she lost her footing and went over the edge. Please, please, you have to help her. I can't reach her. I'm frightened in case she falls."

"Okay, I have the coast guard and the emergency rescue team on the way. Stay on the line with me. Is your friend conversing with you?"

"Yes, her voice is weak. She told me that she's struggling to hang on. Please, help her."

"It would be better if you remained calm. Keep talking to your friend. Reassure her that she will be rescued soon. Can you do that for me?"

"Yes. Please, don't hang up. Stay with me."

"I will. Don't worry about that. Talk to your friend. What's her name?"

"It's Geraldine. Please, you have to help her. She's been through such a traumatic time."

"What's your name?" the controller asked, his voice calming in tone.

"I'm Ruth."

"Okay, Ruth. I'll guide you through this. Do as I've already suggested and talk to your friend. Keep her talking. I'll be right here with you. The teams are on their way. They're close now, I'm tracking them on my screen. We won't let either you or your friend down."

"That's a relief to hear. Okay, I'm going to shout. I'll hold the phone away so I don't deafen you."

The man chuckled. "That's thoughtful of you."

"Geraldine. Can you hear me?"

"Yes, Ruth. Help me. I'm losing my grip."

She gasped and relayed the information to the man on control. "Please, what shall I tell her? How far are the rescue teams now?"

"Five minutes. You're doing so well. Stick with it. Keep reassuring her."

"They'll be here in a minute or two, Geraldine, just hang on tight. We won't let you down."

"I can't hold on much longer, I'm losing my grip, Ruth."

"You have to, sweetheart. For all our sakes," she shouted. Returning the phone to her ear, she asked the control operator, "How long now? I don't think she can hold on much longer. Damn, if only I had a rope. I have one in the car, but it's a good ten-minute walk back. I fear that might be too late." She strained her ears. In the distance, she could hear the faint wail of sirens. "They're here, the cavalry is coming up the hill. Oh, thank goodness."

"That's great to hear. Stay with me, Ruth, right up until the time they find you."

"I will. I'm going to tell Geraldine now." She held the phone away from her and shouted, "Geraldine, stay still, they're almost here. I can hear them coming now."

"Please, tell them to hurry. My hands are slipping."

Something caught Ruth's eye out at sea. It was a small boat; the coastguard had located them. Tears filled her eyes, tears of relief as a helicopter appeared from around the bay. "They're here, Geraldine. They're all around us. Please dig deep and hang in there."

"I'll try. It's so difficult, though. I'm trying to grip the edge so hard my fingernails are snapping off."

"Sod your nails. You can have new ones. I'll even pay for them, love. Just hold on as if your life depends on it." Never a truer word spoken.

Behind her, two burly men arrived in orange coveralls, with ropes over their shoulders.

"Thank goodness. She's down there. I think she must have lost her footing. Here, I almost did the same, please be careful."

A man with a moustache and a kind face smiled and moved her away from the edge. "We'll take it from here. Don't worry, she'll be safe."

"Thank you. Please hurry, she's struggling to hang on."

"Ruth, are you there, Ruth?" the control operator shouted down the line.

She'd forgotten all about him. "I'm here. Sorry, the teams have arrived," she shouted above the noise of the helicopter overhead.

"Okay, Ruth. I'm going to hang up now. Good luck. Your friend is in safe hands."

"Thank you for all your assistance. I couldn't have done this without you."

"Just doing my job. Take care now."

Ruth pressed the End Call button and got down on her knees to hug Ben, tears streaming down her flushed face. "We did it, boy. We saved her."

She watched as a man was lowered from the helicopter. Moments later, he was being winched back up, now grasping tightly to Geraldine.

Ruth waved frantically while Geraldine clung tightly to the man rescuing her.

One of the rescuers stood alongside Ruth and rubbed his hand up and down her arm. "Your call just saved your friend's life. You should be very proud of your actions. Not everyone would have had the gumption to do what you did."

"Thank you. I didn't do anything out of the ordinary. You see, she only got married yesterday."

"Wow, what a way to celebrate," the young rescuer said, laughing.

Ruth shook her head and sighed. "You don't understand. Her husband was killed after the ceremony."

"What? That's unbelievable. Hey, wait a minute, you don't think she was trying to do away with herself, do you?"

Ruth's shoulders met her ears in the deepest shrug she could muster. "I really can't answer that."

"Blimey! Either she's going to be all over you with gratitude or she's going to hate you for the rest of your life."

"Don't. I hadn't thought about that. Let's hope it's the former. What will happen now? Will she be taken to the hospital to get checked over?"

"That's usually the case. We'll wrap things up here. Let me place a call to the helicopter to ensure she's okay and what their next step will be." He turned his back and walked a few feet away from her.

Ruth's gaze drifted back to the helicopter. The rescuer was just pulling Geraldine into the helicopter. She didn't wave back at Ruth. Perhaps Geraldine was too traumatised by her adventure, or maybe not. She pondered what the rescuer had said to her. *Had Geraldine tried to end her life? Was she in such a desperate state to even contemplate that? Had her parents' arguing sent her over the edge? Or was this truly a simple case of Geraldine misjudging her footing during a walk? Perhaps she'd been distracted by the events of yesterday and hadn't noticed where she was treading.*

Ruth would need to find out the truth, if Geraldine was keen to share. If not, the questions would linger while she investigated Bradley's death.

"She's going to the Royal Infirmary. The Accident and Emergency department. Do you need a lift?"

"No. I have my car. I can't thank you enough for saving her. I'll be eternally grateful to you all."

"Let's hope she's as grateful as you," the man said.

She watched him and the other rescuer walk away, his words rattling around in her head. Her gaze rose skyward once more. By now the helicopter was close to dipping around the edge of the bay. Ben was sitting beside her, patiently waiting, seemingly oblivious to what had just taken place. She ruffled his head. "Come on, boy. Let's get you home, and then I'll have to shoot over to the hospital to see if Geraldine is all right."

Ruth was halfway back to the car when her phone rang. The caller ID told her it was Hilary Makey ringing. She finished putting Ben in the car and then leaned against the door to take the call. "Hi, Hils, how are things going?"

"They're all right with me. How's it going with you? Or should I say Geraldine? I've only just heard the damn gossip. I didn't get back from Mum's until late yesterday. Denis filled me in."

"How is your mum?"

"She's fine. Her hip is still sore after the operation, but she's home now. I stocked up the freezer for her and Dad before I left. I bet he'll cremate the meals when he heats them up. He has no idea about what the oven looks like, let alone how to use one."

Ruth smiled. "Typical man, eh? Well, I'm in kind of a rush right now. Would it be all right if I ring you later?"

"It's Am-Dram club tonight, won't you be there?"

Damn! Rubbing a hand over her face, she tried to conjure up a genuine excuse not to attend, but her mind was that fuzzy she couldn't come up with one. "Of course. I'll fill you in later. See you at seven in the town hall then."

"Don't hang up, Ruth, are you sure you're okay? You sound a bit distant."

"It's been an eventful morning so far. I'll be there, I promise."

"See you later. Take care of yourself until then."

"I will, Hils. Thanks for ringing."

After ending the call, she inhaled a large lungful of the fresh sea breeze and hopped back in the car. A few minutes later, she had dropped Ben at home, and fed and watered him before she drove to the hospital.

It was a half-hour journey. The Accident and Emergency Department was relatively quiet. She walked up to the blonde receptionist. "Hello, my friend was brought in by a rescue team via helicopter. Is it possible to see her?"

"Ah, I know the lady you're talking about. Wait here. I'll go and check for you."

Ruth paced the area for a bit and then stopped to read some of the announcements pinned to the noticeboard. She smiled when the one she had posted herself caught her eye. It was regarding the Am-Dram club she'd formed a few years earlier. They were always on the lookout for talented volunteers to join them. She loved spending time with the group, each of them slightly different in character. She couldn't wait to meet up with them that night. By then she'd need the escapism she always felt when she attended the club.

"Hello there." The receptionist suddenly appeared beside her, startling her a little.

Ruth placed a hand over her heart. "Sorry, you made me jump. I was miles away."

"No problem. If you'd like to come with me, I'll take you to see your friend. She was very lucky by all accounts."

"She was. I was told by her parents she'd gone up there so I set off to look for her. My dog actually located her. He sniffed the edge as if something was there. I called Geraldine's name and that's when I heard her faint cry. If the rescuers hadn't arrived when they had... well, I can't even imagine what would have happened to her."

"Must have been a horrendous ordeal for the pair of you. Here we are." She swept back a curtain to reveal Geraldine sitting up in bed.

Ruth rushed forward and hugged her dear friend. "Oh, Geraldine, I'm so glad you're all right. What happened?"

Geraldine's eyes appeared glazed. *Is she in shock? Have the doctors given her medication?*

"I don't know."

Ruth didn't push her for more answers. It was obvious she was struggling after her ordeal. "Have they contacted your parents?"

Geraldine shrugged. "I don't know and I don't care. I wish everyone would stop bombarding me with questions. All I want to do is curl up and sleep."

"I can understand you being tired after your adventure, but your parents will be worried about you. Please, let me ring them?"

Geraldine stared at the pattern on the blanket covering her.

"Ger, please. Don't shut me out. I want to help you. I can't do that if you won't open up to me."

Geraldine slowly turned to face her. "I'm lost without him."

Hearing those four words made Ruth's head spin. *Oh no, had she intended to kill herself? Surely she wouldn't have cried out for help if that was her intention, would she?*

"I know, sweetie. It will get easier, I promise. It's been less than twenty-four hours since…he died."

"I know. What will I do now? How will I cope? We had so many plans, and now they've all disintegrated, shattered into tiny pieces when he fell from the turret yesterday. How am I ever going to cope without him by my side?"

"I can't deny it's not going to be difficult, Ger. Your friends and family will rally around to help you. You can be sure of that."

"Will they? All I saw yesterday was pity in their eyes. I don't want to be pitied. I'm still relatively young. I should be on my honeymoon right now with the man I love. Instead, he's lying in a fridge at the morgue." Tears streamed down her face.

"I know. My heart bleeds for you. We'll get through this together. I won't desert you in your hour of need. None of us will. I'm going to ring your parents."

Geraldine's hand grabbed hers. "No. I don't want them here. I'm sick to death of their continual bickering. All they do is constantly throw the divorce card at each other. Why the heck don't they go ahead and do it? They don't care about me. If they did, they wouldn't keep tearing shreds out of each other. Why? Why do they insist on remaining married? That's not what life should be about, is it? We deserve to be happy in this life, not miserable all the time."

"I understand what you're saying. Have they always been that way? I've only met them a few times, and they always seem to get on one another's nerves."

"Since I was a kid. Their attitude to marriage should have put me off wanting to get married myself. It didn't. I loved Bradley so much…

74

was going to spend the rest of my life with him, and now…he's gone. How am I going to cope without him?"

"You just will. We'll all be here to support you. You're not going to go through this alone, I promise you."

Geraldine snuggled down into the bed and rested her head against the pillow. Sighing heavily, she said, "I need to go to sleep now. Thank you for rescuing me. I love you dearly, Ruth."

"Give me a shout, day or night, if you ever want to chat."

"I will. I'm tired now."

Geraldine drifted off to sleep.

Ruth pulled back the curtain to leave as a young female doctor was arriving.

"Ah, I see the patient has gone off to sleep."

"Have you given her some medication? Is she going to be all right, Doc?"

"Yes, she needs to rest. Don't worry, she's going to be fine. A few cuts and bruises and possibly a bruised rib, but nothing more than that. Were you the person who called the rescuers in?"

"Yes. One of them put the idea in my head that she did this intentionally. Do you think that's possible?"

"Who knows? She gave me some background; she's been through a tough ordeal. The brain often reacts differently to the heart in such instances. We'll keep her under observation for a day or two. Maybe she'll open up to either me or one of my colleagues in that time. I wouldn't like to be in her shoes, that's for sure. Newly married and widowed after only a few hours. That type of situation has to mess with your head, doesn't it?"

"Is it worth me sticking around?"

The doctor smiled and shook her head. "Not really. She'll be out for the count for a few hours, maybe you can return then."

"I will. Thank you for taking care of her."

"It's our pleasure. Let's hope the enforced rest puts her on the road to recovery."

"Here's hoping. Can I leave you my number? Perhaps a member of your team could ring me if there is any change with her."

"That's a good idea."

Ruth opened her bag and pulled out the pouch she kept her business cards in and handed one to the doctor.

"Detective Agency?"

"I'm a private investigator."

"Call me nosy, if you like. But does this mean you'll be investigating her husband's death?"

"She's asked me to. I'll do my best without treading on the local police's toes."

"She's going to need someone she trusts on her side in the foreseeable future."

"I'll be there for her, you can be sure of that, Doctor."

"She's very lucky to have such a caring friend. I must get on. I'll leave your card with the receptionist with strict instructions to ring you when she wakes up."

"You're very kind."

Ruth left the hospital and headed back to the house. She made a slight detour on the way to let Valerie and Ted Cruise know what was going on.

The couple were both shocked to learn the news.

"I need to go and see her. To be with her," Valerie whispered.

"There really is no point in either of you going there now. She's been sedated and will be asleep for a good few hours yet. I needed to bring you up to date before I go back home."

"Thank you for being such a kind friend to her, Ruth. We really appreciate it, don't we, Ted?" Valerie held her hand out to her husband.

He took it, pulled his wife close and buried his head in her neck. "Our poor baby. Where were we when she needed us?" he mumbled, his tone full of what sounded like remorse.

"No more recriminations. Please, all I ask is that you consider Geraldine's feelings and what she must be going through from now on. The next few days and weeks are possibly going to be the toughest of her life. She'll be relying on you both to be there for her, not squabbling as you've been doing the past few days."

Valerie nodded. "You're right. We've always been the same. We don't mean anything by it. We love each other dearly."

"What? Then why? Why do you insist on flinging the divorce card at each other all the time? Can't you see how that looks to Geraldine?"

Valerie held her head in shame, they both did. "We'll reconsider our actions, we promise," Valerie said.

Dumbstruck, Ruth shrugged and left the house, unsure what she could add further after such a shocking admission. Right up until the day she died, she would never, ever fully understand what went on in people's heads.

She returned home and spent the afternoon preparing the Sunday roast for when James finished his shift. She almost sliced through her finger a couple of times when her mind drifted back to the events of what could only be described as a traumatic twenty-four hours.

During the afternoon, she received several calls from other members of the Am-Dram club, asking if she was going to attend the weekly meeting that evening. She sat at the kitchen table after her chores were completed with a cup of latte in her hand and contemplated what a wonderful community she belonged to. Even if there was a murderer in their midst.

CHAPTER 6

THAT EVENING, when James returned home, Ruth resisted the temptation to pump him for information about Geraldine's case the minute he stepped through the front door. Instead, she served up the dinner she'd slaved over for hours and recapped the events of what had gone on up on the clifftop.

"Are you serious?" James asked, his jaw dropping after she'd finished.

"Deadly serious. I thought she was a goner. I was so scared. I think if the rescuers hadn't shown up when they had, the town would have been having a double funeral in the coming weeks."

"How awful. You don't think she meant it to happen, do you?"

"I have my doubts. The thought never crossed my mind until one of the rescuers mentioned it. Then when I visited her at the hospital, she was, well, frankly, talking weirdly. I wasn't sure if it was the medication they'd given her. I don't know is the honest answer. What I can say for definite is that I'm concerned about her. I believe Bradley's death has affected her far more than any of us had first realised."

"That's so sad. Let's hope finding the person responsible will give her the peace of mind to continue with her life."

Ruth held her crossed fingers up in the air. "I know I shouldn't be asking, but is there any news on that front?"

James tilted his head at her and closed one of his eyes. "You're right, you shouldn't be asking. I'm not dealing with the case, you know that, love. Not that I would divulge any information even if I was. Are you going out this evening?"

"Yes, I've had several calls today from the group, pleading with me to attend."

"I'm not surprised. Most of them are as nosy as you and probably want to hear first-hand how the murder came about."

She swiped him across the top of the arm. "Cheeky sod. There's nothing wrong with being inquisitive. It's how we learn about life and what it has to throw at us."

"Yeah, if you say so. Well, if you're going out later, I'll take Ben for a run down by the river."

Ben whined from his bed in the corner. "I know a certain dog who would appreciate that. I shouldn't be late back, probably be home about nine."

He reached across the table and covered her hand with his. "Take as long as you need. You deserve to have a good time after what you've had to contend with in the last day or so."

"Thanks. Although, I think for once, I'd much rather be at home with you tonight than going over and over the ordeal, or should that be ordeals?"

A COUPLE OF HOURS LATER, Ruth kissed James farewell and made her way on foot down to the town hall a few roads from the house.

The rest of the group were all there, gathered around the large table where they either hashed out plans or created the costumes for the shows they put on for the townsfolk. Usually it was a fun-filled evening. However, by the serious expression on each of her friend's faces, Ruth got the impression the next few hours were going to be long and drawn out.

"Come, sit next to me." Hilary yanked the chair out beside her.

"Hi, everyone. I'll have to see how I go this evening. If the hospital rings, I'll have to shoot off. Just pre-warning you."

Several of the group gasped.

"Hospital? What do you mean?" Gemma Isaac, the local hairdresser, asked through the long veil hanging over her face that she laughingly called an 'en trend' fringe.

Ruth spent the next ten minutes recounting the adventure she and Geraldine had lived that morning.

"Is she all right?" Gemma asked, her eyes watering with concern.

"I hope she will be. Put it this way, I wouldn't want to be in her shoes over the next few weeks. I'll be there to support her. I hope the whole community gives her the support she needs as well."

"We will. Maybe we can set up some kind of charity or fund for her," Hilary suggested.

The group murmured in agreement around the table.

"What an excellent idea," Steven Swanson, the props manager, agreed. "Why don't we put on a special event? Let me think about that one for a while, see what set designs we have at our disposal, and I'll get back to you."

Lynn Harris caught Ruth's attention by rolling her eyes up to the ceiling. "That's a nice idea, Steven; however, we need to get down to the nitty-gritty and ask Ruth what *her* intentions are."

"My intentions? In what respect, Lynn?"

"Workwise. Don't tell me Geraldine hasn't asked you to investigate the crime?"

"She has as it happens. I'm willing to do it free of charge, too. The trouble is, I have my nemesis in the police to contend with."

Lynn sucked in her bottom lip and chewed on it for a moment or two. "Inspector Littlejohn, I take it?"

"Yep. The one and only. You of all people know the confrontations we've had over the years. Can't say I'm looking forward to going into battle with her on this one. There's no way I'll back down, not when Geraldine is going to be relying heavily on my input."

Lynn nodded. She was a cherished friend who often showed up at the detective agency to volunteer her secretarial services free of charge, to break up the monotony of being 'just a housewife' as she put it. Her services had proved invaluable to Ruth when she'd first set up the agency. Despite Ruth insisting she should put Lynn on the payroll since the business was now more buoyant, Lynn refused to let Ruth pay her, quoting that getting paid would take the enjoyment out of the job. She drove Ruth to distraction with that way of thinking. At Christmas, Ruth always slipped a little something extra in Lynn's card, whether it was a voucher for a spa day or tickets to a concert she'd been raving about, because at the end of the day, Ruth was one of life's givers.

"You go, girl. I have no doubt that your determination and stubbornness will come up with the answers soon."

Ruth should have been taken aback by what Lynn said. She wasn't. Instead, she laughed. "I'll take that as a backhanded compliment."

Lynn winked. "Of course. I have every faith in you." She leaned forward in her chair and whispered, "Do you really think there's a killer living amongst us?"

She shrugged and said in a hushed voice, "Who knows? We could be looking at an out-of-towner who showed up to attend the wedding with one intention in mind…to kill Bradley. I want to get today over with, make sure Geraldine is all right before I truly start digging."

"But if it was someone from out of town, they'd be long gone by now, surely?"

"You're right. However, there's always some form of trail, you know that, right? Be it a paper trail or someone might have overheard a conversation on the day of the wedding. Wherever the trail starts, I'll be on it like a dog with a bone, I assure you."

"Hey, you two, let us in on the secret?" Hilary called out.

"It's nothing. Just discussing when Lynn can come in and give me a hand at the agency. Certainly nothing for you to worry about," she added, putting Hilary in her place.

Once the interest in the murder had died down, everyone got their heads together to come up with an idea for the added show to raise money for Geraldine. They were already knee-deep in preparing for their main show, which was due to take place at the end of the summer. *The Sound of Music* was much anticipated by all those connected with the Am-Dram club; it was an all-time favourite that hadn't been performed in decades. Now they had another show to think about and all that it entailed.

Ideas were thin on the ground that evening. Steven showed his frustration by drawing a close to the meeting barely two hours after it had started. While the others were upset by the decision, Ruth felt grateful as most of the evening had put her in the limelight with the others demanding to know the ins and outs of a cat's bottom, to do with the case. Ruth struggled to answer the questions bombarding her from the word go because it was just too soon to answer any of them.

At nine o'clock, Ruth took a leisurely walk back to the cottage. It was a warm evening, even though the sky was full of white fluffy clouds. At the bottom of her road, a few of her neighbours gathered around, nattering over the fence between two houses. She waved as she passed and said good evening. They all appeared embarrassed when they responded. It was obvious what they were gossiping about. Her heart went out to Geraldine. She would have to contend with people talking behind her back for months to come—sadly, that was a given in small towns such as this.

A few doors down, a light was on in the run-down cottage her sister and her husband had just bought and were in the throes of renovating. She knocked on the front door. It was ajar, so she pushed it open and poked her head into the stripped room. "Yoo-hoo, anyone here?"

Her sister appeared from the adjoining room, dressed in white denim dungarees covered in plaster and splodges of differently coloured paint. "Hey, I was going to ring you later. Come in if you're not wearing anything decent; otherwise, I'd stay out there if I were you."

Ruth laughed. "I'm half-decent, does that count? How are things going?"

"So-so. I think it has finally dawned on Keith what a mammoth task this project is."

"Oi, I heard that. Hi, Ruth. Feel free to don some grubby clothes and lend a hand," Carolyn's husband shouted from the adjoining room.

"Erm…thanks for the offer, hon, but don't be offended if I decline," Ruth shouted back.

Keith mumbled something indecipherable and started banging pipework again.

"Oops, I think I've upset him. What's he doing?"

Moving a few steps closer and lowering her voice, Carolyn said, "Putting in the central heating. Told me it would be a doddle. Have you ever heard of an electrician doing a plumber's job?"

"Can't say I have. Did he think it would save you guys some money?"

"That's exactly why he's doing it. The only thing is, it's taking twice as long, and I predict the job is far messier than if he'd paid a professional plumber to do it."

"Men, eh? They think they know best, but in the end they're always proved wrong. You need to learn to put your foot down. It's your money as well invested in this place."

"We've had that argument dozens of times before, you know that. I let him get on with it."

"That's not fair on you in the end, Carolyn. Adds to the stress of the job in hand, doesn't it?"

"I know. We'll sit down and discuss things once this place is done and dusted. It's a good job our relationship is solid, otherwise we'd be on seriously dodgy ground by now. Anyway, enough about this place. How did the wedding go yesterday?"

Ruth winced. She should have realised Carolyn and Keith wouldn't have heard the news if they'd been wrapped up in their own cocoon renovating the cottage. "Damn, you won't have heard."

"Heard what? What's wrong with your face all of a sudden?"

"There was a murder up at the hall yesterday."

Carolyn let out a yelp and dropped the paintbrush she was holding. "Really? Who?"

"Only the goddamn groom."

"Keith, get in here. You need to hear this."

Her husband appeared in the doorway, his face covered in sawdust. "What? I'm busy, you know that, Carolyn."

"Ruth has something to tell us. It's important, love."

He came closer to them and crossed his arms. "Go on, you've got my attention."

"Don't be sarcastic and listen. Go on, Ruth, tell us how it happened?"

"How what happened?" Keith asked, confused.

"Shh, just listen," Carolyn reprimanded sternly.

Ruth sighed and went over the events of the previous day which her sister and brother-in-law had missed due to their determination to get the renovations completed before the end of the year, doing most of the work while the good weather was still with them.

"That's simply dreadful. Poor Geraldine, I bet she's beside herself," Carolyn said, resting against the bare wall behind her for support.

"She is. Actually, she's in hospital right now."

"What?" Keith asked. "Why?"

Ruth recapped the events that led up to Geraldine's admittance to hospital. Her sister and brother-in-law were stunned again for the second time in as many minutes.

Carolyn shook her head. "Did she try and take her own life?"

"I don't think so. I've mentioned it to numerous people now, and that's the response I've received from most of them. The thing is, she cried out for help and was clinging on to the cliff when Ben and I arrived. If her intention was to throw herself off, wouldn't she have gone the whole hog? Even if the cliff had broken her fall? Maybe that's the investigator in me thinking along those lines."

"Hmm, you could be right in that assumption," Carolyn agreed. "Poor thing, she's going to need your help more than ever at the moment, Ruth. That's going to be a huge burden on your shoulders. Are her parents still around?"

"Yes, what use they're going to be, I really can't say. They constantly bicker. I had a chat with them this morning. Not sure if they'll be able to put their differences aside for the sake of their daughter or not. They promised me they would, but words come cheaply to some people, you know that as well as I do."

"Shame on them. They should be able to set aside their differences, especially at a time like this, for Geraldine's sake. Thank goodness she has you as a dear friend who she can rely on. Do you have any ideas who would want Bradley dead?"

"Sadly, there are no clues at this time. I forgot to mention that my nemesis on the force is in charge of this investigation."

"That's a bummer. What's her problem anyway?"

"I suppose she hates the fact that I've beaten her by solving more crimes in the past."

"Egg-on-face syndrome perhaps?" Carolyn suggested.

"Possibly."

"Right, ladies, as much as I'd like to hang around and gossip, I have pipes to bend and creepy corners I need to get into while the light is still with me." Keith backed away from them and returned to the other room.

"He's probably thankful that I haven't murdered him during this renovation. The subject was probably too near the mark for him."

Ruth laughed at Carolyn's admission. "You're probably right. You two are all right, though, aren't you? I know how stressful it's been over the last couple of months."

The whole family, Carolyn, Keith and their two boys, Ian and Robin, had been living in the back garden in a caravan for the past six months since they'd sold their previous house. Carolyn often complained that caravan life was getting on everyone's nerves, which was why she and Keith had started working extra hours on the renovations. Her heart went out to her sister. This was Keith's dream, to have the quintessential cottage in a thriving community. He loved the character these buildings had and was supercharged with enthusiasm to bring that character to life in this beautiful building, no matter what the cost, either financially or emotionally.

"We're fine. A few niggles as we get closer to the finishing line, nothing major."

"Finishing line? Are you kidding me? This place looks like it has had a bomb dropped on it in the blitz."

"You are funny. It's not as bad as some renovation projects I've seen on TV. We're sort of enjoying the process. The novelty is wearing a little thin now, but at least we can visualise the end result. I struggled with that aspect up until last week. I'd offer to show you around, but you'd get really filthy."

"I'll take your word for that. You don't look that much further on than the last time I popped my head in a few weeks ago."

"We are. It's the heating that's been the problem in the last few weeks. Keith is doing his best to hide the pipes—not always easy when you have cob walls that are sometimes a foot thick in places."

"Ouch, I bet. All right, I'm going to love you and leave you. I need to write down a few notes before I start the investigation in earnest tomorrow. Give my love to the boys. Here's a thought... You put them to work for their pocket money. Tell them if they want to live in a house with this much character you all need to go back in time to when it was built. Didn't they use boys of around ten to do the dirty work back then?"

"You're a harsh woman. They'd have a fit and probably report us to Social Services if the idea ever left my lips." Carolyn laughed and waved her off.

Ruth chuckled and fastened the gate. "Take care. Don't work too hard. I'm dying to see the results of all your hard work. When is that likely to be?"

"We're hoping to be in before Crimbo."

"Christmas? Ah, but which year?"

"You cheeky mare. You'll be eating your words along with the turkey on Christmas Day when you're sitting at our table eating all the trimmings with the rest of the family, you'll see."

"I'll look forward to that. I'm going home now to mark it on my calendar."

Carolyn's mouth turned down at the sides. "Blimey, we'd better get back to it then. Ring you soon."

Ruth chuckled and left her sister to return to the dust and

disgusting paint fumes. She strolled down the rest of the quiet road, one half of her mind on Christmas and the other half with Geraldine. What kind of Christmas would it be for her this year?

James and Ben were sitting in the lounge when she arrived home.

"Crikey, I didn't realise you were actually going to be playing around with the set tonight down at the club." He pointed at her hair.

She tapped at her fringe and watched the dust fall in front of her. "No, this isn't from the club. I stopped off to see how Carolyn and Keith were getting on."

"Damn, I keep meaning to drop in and see if they need a hand. Just been up to my neck in work lately."

"Well, if things die down for you over the coming weeks, they could sure use some help. They're talking about having us all around there for Christmas dinner."

"They are? How far along are they?" He patted the couch for her to sit beside him.

She dumped her bag on the floor and collapsed next to him. He wrapped an arm around her shoulder, and Ben jumped up on the couch on the other side of her. She ruffled Ben's head. "Cheeky, boy. Well, to me, it doesn't look as if they've made any headway at all, not since I popped in a few weeks ago. Keith's putting in the central heating. Carolyn said all the work is happening under the floorboards et cetera, so it's hard to tell if they've made any great strides with the renovation. As you can see, it's still dusty as hell in there. I dread to think what state their lungs will be in by the end of it."

"Ah, the trials and tribulations of renovating a beautiful old cottage. We were lucky this place was already done when we moved in. Do you think they're trying to emulate our cottage?"

"I'm not sure about that. They're just trying to make it habitable for them and the boys. Carolyn said living in the caravan is beginning to take its toll on them all."

He leaned forward and narrowed his eyes. "I know that tone. There's something you're not saying."

Ruth smiled. "You think you know me so well. I was just wondering if we could offer them shelter during the autumn and winter. It might give them the impetus to get a wriggle on if they get a decent night's sleep and they're not riddled with guilt because of the boys."

"Hmm...I would have thought the opposite. Living in the caravan would give them the impetus they needed to get the job finished earlier."

She shook her head. "You're a harsh man at times, James Winchester."

"But you love me, right?" He lowered his mouth to meet hers.

After they'd shared a satisfying kiss, she withdrew and looked him in the eye. "Can I suggest it to them?"

His shoulders rose to meet his ears. "Do I really have a choice in the matter?"

"It might not come to that anyway. Knowing how independent Carolyn is, she'll probably turn me down."

She might, but the boys will jump at the chance to wreak havoc around here, teasing Ben and shouting while they play computer games on our TV."

Ruth shuddered at the thought of their tranquillity being disrupted for months on end. "Okay, you win. I'll only suggest it if we have a really snowy winter, how about that?"

He squeezed her to him and pecked her on the forehead. "That's a deal."

She flew out of the chair to collect her pen and paper from the sideboard. "Good. Now that's out of the way, I need to make some notes about where my investigation should begin."

"Do you need a hand? Unofficially, of course."

"I was hoping you'd say that. I want to draw up a list of possible witnesses." She retook her seat and poised her pen ready.

"What? You do realise how many people were at the wedding, don't you?"

"Yep, around a hundred. I can't say I'm looking forward to the task in hand, but needs must. Now, who can you remember being there?"

Together, over the course of the next few hours, they managed to list over eighty names. That meant she wouldn't be able to interview at least twenty people, not unless she got hold of the wedding list from the wedding planner. Now, why hadn't she thought about that earlier? It had been a tiring weekend, and she'd been racing around from pillar to post in one way or another.

The final thing she did before she turned in for the evening was ring the hospital to see how Geraldine was doing. The ward sister said she was sleeping. Apparently, she had been extremely tearful during the day. Her state of mind would be reassessed in the morning before any further decisions would be made about whether she'd be discharged or remain in hospital under supervision. *Does that mean the doctor thought she'd attempted suicide as well?* Her heart went out to her old school friend. Between them, this was by far the toughest situation life had thrown at them over the years. Her only thought now was whether Geraldine was strong enough to pull through what was about to be thrown at her over the next week or so.

CHAPTER 7

RUTH WOKE up to the birds singing gaily and the warmth of the early morning sun. James had left for work hours before. She stretched out to find Ben lying on his side. He had replaced James on the bed.

She turned over and flung an arm over him and kissed him on the head. "Morning, sunshine, how are you today?"

He moaned and extended all four paws out in front of him.

After a few minutes of snuggling into his fur, she bit the bullet and got up, flinging back the quilt so it intentionally covered Ben. He jumped off the bed and sneezed with excitement, the way he always did in the morning when he was eager to go out.

Ruth slipped on her pink towelling robe and drifted down the stairs to let Ben out. She switched on the kettle and popped a few pieces of bread in the toaster while she waited for her four-legged companion to do his business in the garden.

She thought about the day ahead of her and groaned. Ben sauntered in through the back door just as the toast popped up. She poured the water over her coffee granules and buttered her toast, then she took ten minutes out to eat her breakfast. It was only seven-thirty, after all.

Breakfast eaten, she ventured upstairs again to shower and dress.

Half an hour later, she was ready to leave the house, her constant companion by her side. He went everywhere with her and loved riding in the car—it was the highlight of his day.

Ruth unlocked the office door and settled down behind her clutter-free desk. Tidy desk, tidy mind, as the saying went. She'd always adhered to that, not only for her own well-being but also in case any clients walked in off the street. It was far better to work on one file that she could flip shut at a moment's notice than work with several different cases open at the same time.

She felt daunted. So many people to interview she really didn't have a clue where to begin. Whilst she waited for a bright idea to spark, she made herself her second coffee of the day. Always far wiser to contemplate the mammoth task ahead of her with a double dose of caffeine coursing through her veins.

Suitably invigorated, she took out her pad and ran a finger down the list she'd created with James the previous evening but then paused. "Nope, the first job is to seek out the wedding planner. Did Geraldine even have one?" She had her doubts as Geraldine had told her that she'd arranged everything herself. But there must be a list of sorts lying around, for the wedding dinner perhaps? She picked up the phone and called Lady Falkirk, hoping she could shed some light on what was troubling her.

"Lady Falkirk is indisposed at the present time. May I help you at all, Miss?" Lady Falkirk's butler asked her.

"You probably can, Mr Wells. I was hoping to get my hands on a list of the people who attended the wedding."

"I'm not sure there is such a thing. I can ask Lady Falkirk once she's finished her meeting and call you back, if that would help?"

"Perfect. I know Geraldine arranged most things but I would've thought she would have handed over a list or some form of seating plan for the guests. Or am I wrong about that?"

"Possibly. I wouldn't like to say. I'll get back to you as soon as I've found out. Good morning, Miss Morgan."

"You're very kind. Thank you, Mr Wells."

Feeling disappointed, her enthusiasm dashed, Ruth sat back in her chair and tapped her pen on the desk. This little problem needn't delay her. After all, she had the list she had created with James that she could use for now.

The next hour consisted of Ruth looking through the phone book, obtaining the numbers of the people she needed to call. She then worked her way through the list, asking those she spoke to whether they had either seen or overheard anything suspicious during the wedding that she should know about, specifically before Bradley's death. Although, she was willing to listen to anything anyone said they'd heard after the incident, too. *Grasping at straws there, girl.* She might have been, but what else was there on the table for her to use?

Getting nowhere fast, her spirits had dropped to rock bottom, but a call she received halfway through the morning lifted her mood once more.

"Miss Morgan? It's Timothy Wells from Carmel Cove Hall here. I have the information you need. It's a little tatty around the edges but it's still decipherable. Would you like to collect it?"

"Thank you. That's wonderful news. I'll be right there."

"See you soon in that case."

The butler ended the call first. Ruth grabbed her handbag and Ben's leash from the nearby chair. Ben was on his feet in a flash, spinning in circles all the way to the door. "All right, boy, I suppose we'll be able to fit in a run at the park on the way back if you're super good in the car."

After hearing the two most popular words in his vocabulary, *park* and *car*, Ben woofed excitedly.

She laughed and ruffled his head then stepped out of the office. He ran to the car and bounced on the spot while she opened the door. She placed him in the harness and laid his leash on the seat beside him, then she jumped behind the steering wheel and drove up to Carmel Cove Hall.

Mr Wells must have heard the car approach because he appeared on the steps of the hall before she had the chance to get out of her vehicle. He strode across the gravel and motioned for her to open the window.

"Hello, there. I can't tell you how much I appreciate this, Mr Wells. Thank you so much."

"All part of the job, Miss. Good luck with your investigation."

"Thank you. I know Geraldine will be super grateful, too, when I let her know what you've done for us."

His stern, officious face softened slightly. "Ah, how is Miss Geraldine? Did I hear she was taken to hospital yesterday?"

"You did. They're taking good care of her. I think she'll be home in the next day or two."

"Glad to hear it. Please send her my regards and best wishes."

"I will." She waved the list in her hand and smiled. "Thank you again for this. I'm sure it will come in handy."

"I hope it helps." The stern expression reappeared on his face. "I hope you find the person responsible for the murder."

"I'm sure I will. I have a reputation to uphold in the community, Mr Wells."

"Indeed. So long for now. You know where I am if you should need any further assistance, Miss Morgan."

"Thank you. That's very kind of you, sir."

He nodded stiffly and strode away from the car and in through the grand entrance to the hall.

"Right, that's work out the way. It's playtime now, Ben. Just a quick one, though, all right?"

Ben moaned and paced the back seat until they reached the large park close to the centre of town. She trusted Ben off-lead and watched him sniff the ground ahead of her. She threw his ball once she got his attention, and he galloped after it, his tail doing a great impression of a helicopter's blades.

Another dog approached. Ben was instantly attracted to the poodle strutting her stuff around him.

"Oops, we'd better drag them apart before we end up with a pack of Labradoodles on our hands," Ruth said to the poodle's owner, chortling.

"Oh my. Wouldn't that be simply adorable?" the middle-aged lady said.

Ruth knew most of the people in the town who exercised their dogs at the park but failed to recognise this lady. "Are you new to the area?"

"Yes, we moved into the old station house a few days ago."

"How wonderful. That place is in dire need of renovation. What plans do you have for it? Sorry if you think I'm being nosy." She offered her hand for the woman to shake. "I'm Ruth Morgan, the local private investigator."

"Wow, a Miss Marple in our midst. I'm Cynthia Jackson by the way. Just a general renovation."

"Hardly. But I do have a good track record, not wishing to blow my own trumpet."

"Well, if you can't blow your own trumpet, others aren't going to do it for you. Don't take this the wrong way, but I hope I don't ever need your services in the future."

They both laughed. "You'd be surprised the number of people who say that and then eventually seek out my help."

"Gosh, I hope not. As far as I know, my husband adores me, worships the ground beneath my feet and has never cheated on me in the past. Isn't that the majority of cases you cover, ones of infidelity?"

"Mostly. I'm glad your husband is one of the men who appear to be in the minority around these parts. I'm dealing with a far more serious case right now."

Cynthia peered over her shoulder briefly then leaned in. "Not that awful murder that happened over the weekend?"

"Oh, you've heard about that. It was my friend's husband."

Cynthia gasped, and her poodle looked up at her out of concern. "No, that poor woman. Fancy getting married one minute and seeing your husband splayed out in front of you the next, his neck broken."

"You seem very well-informed, Cynthia."

"I might have overheard a conversation between a few of the locals at the supermarket yesterday."

"Ah, I see. I know how hard it is to escape the local gossip in a small town like this."

"Which leads me to ask, it shouldn't be too difficult to ascertain who the killer is, should it?"

"Maybe. I've only just started the investigation this morning, although saying that, as with all weddings, there will always be a number of out-of-towners on the wedding guest list."

"That's true. Well, either way, I wish you every success tracking down the killer, dear. I must confess, I did hesitate and question if we'd made the right choice coming here after I heard about the incident."

"Honestly, things like this rarely happen around here. Hey, if you need any advice with the renovations, my sister and her husband are in the throes of renovating their quaint cottage. Maybe it would be good if you met up with them, when you both have a few spare moments that is."

"Sounds like fun. How far are they into their renovation?"

"They're doing everything themselves. They're hoping to finish by Christmas. I think they meant this year, not next. Although looking at the state of the place, I'm not so sure. Have you ever renovated a house before?"

"Oh yes, my husband, Michael, and I are aware of the pitfalls. That's why I'm insisting that Michael is specifically hands-off with this project. I want this place done and dusted in a matter of weeks, a couple of months at the latest. Our last project was a manor house with sixty rooms. Far too big for the pair of us. We made a handsome profit out of it, though, so mustn't grumble. We've put the rest of the money in a pension pot, ready for when we can kick back and enjoy life. Until then, Michael insists he has one more renovation in him. I'm going along with that for now, anything for a quiet life. Are you married, dear?"

Ruth raised her hand in front of her. "That's a sore point. My boyfriend is trying to get me down the aisle, but I'm struggling with that idea at present. I love him dearly, just not feeling comfortable about committing."

"My, it's usually the other way around in a relationship. Don't you want the big wedding under your belt?"

"Not really, no."

"Oh my, then you do have a problem." Cynthia sniggered.

Ruth smiled and shrugged. "So it would appear. It was lovely speaking to you. I hope you settle in well. No doubt I'll see you around in the future."

"Do you have a card on you?"

"Of course. Ring me if you need to know anything about the town et cetera." She handed Cynthia a card.

Cynthia looked at the card and chuckled. "Excellent! I feel as though I'm ahead of the game. You never know when you'll need your own PI."

Ruth slipped the leash on Ben, who was still paying far too much attention to Cynthia's poodle, and walked back to the car.

That afternoon, she continued to ring more people on her list without obtaining any significant results. In the end, she closed the office at five, earlier than usual, and went home.

James was in the kitchen, making coffee when she entered the room. She kissed him on the cheek. "How was your day?"

"Busy as usual. You look ticked off. Everything all right?"

"So-so. Frustrating day on my part, I'd guess you'd call it. I feel like a duck paddling fast to get away from an alligator and not getting very far."

He laughed and placed a comforting arm around her shoulder. "You'll get there. Something will eventually slip into place, it always does with you. You've got this."

"Sometimes a very special police officer gives me a clue if we're working on the same case."

He unhooked his arm and stepped away from her. "I can't keep doing that, Ruth. You know how close I got to getting caught last time I offered to lend you a hand. At the end of the day, my bosses are going to figure out where you get your 'valuable information' from, and it's going to be my head on the chopping block, not yours."

"But, surely, you want to know what happened to Bradley as much as I do, don't you?"

"Of course I do. That's kind of stating the obvious, but there are procedures in place to prevent us from telling every Tom, Dick or Harry the ins and outs of a case."

"I dispute that. You've never handed me anything on a plate. You might have led me to a possible suspect's door before or dropped a hint as to what a suspect's motive was that initiated a shake-up in my powers of deduction, but nothing more than that. I'm quite offended that you'd even suggest otherwise." Ruth crossed her arms in defiance and tapped her foot.

"Now don't go getting all prissy on me. I know what you're like when you don't get your own way."

"Prissy? *Prissy?* What are you talking about? Since when was stating facts classed as being *prissy?* You need to take a good look at yourself in the mirror sometimes, James. Take a look at that self-righteous chip sitting on your shoulder. And you wonder why I refuse to marry you."

His mouth dropped open. She realised she'd overstepped the mark, but there was no going back now. She turned on her heel and picked up her car keys. Ben took that as a sign to follow her. She bent down and kissed the top of his head. "You stay here, boy. Mummy needs to go out for some fresh air."

Ben began to howl when she walked away from him, the heart-rending noise tugging on her heartstrings. She reached for his leash and beckoned him. Together they trotted towards the back door.

"I swear that damn dog means more to you than I do. One of these days you're going to come home and find all my stuff missing, Ruth. There's only so much a man will take from the woman he loves, especially if that love and respect isn't reciprocated."

Seething, she turned to glare at him, ready to give him a furious rebuttal. Instead, she shook her head, tugged on Ben's leash and slammed the door behind her.

"Men! Who the heck do they think they are? Whoever wrote that damn book about men being from Mars was spot on. We're poles apart at times. Ugh...there's no way I'd marry a man who didn't think I loved him—or share a bed with him in the future either."

With Ben loaded into the back seat of the car, she drove around town for about half an hour just to try to cool her temper. Then, not wishing to go home to embark on round two with James, she headed over to Geraldine's house, wondering if she was home yet. She slapped her thigh for being too wrapped up in her work which had made her forget to catch up on her friend's well-being. *There I go again, having a pop at myself when all I've been doing all day is working on Geraldine's case. Lighten up, girl, for goodness' sake.*

Geraldine hugged her like there was no tomorrow. Maybe in her world there wasn't at the moment. "Are you alone?"

"Yes, although Ben is in the car."

"No. I won't have that. You know he's always welcome in this house. Go get him. I could do with a warm snuggle from him. I'll put the kettle on."

"Okay. I'll be back in a tick." Ruth returned to the car and unhooked Ben from his harness and slipped his leash around his head. "You're lucky she adores you, handsome boy."

He licked her face in response and leapt out of the car.

They entered the back door to Geraldine's house again. "Are your parents not around?"

"I sent them off to the pub. Their arguing was getting me down again. I wish they'd either pack it in or go home. I can't stand their petty bickering. It wears you down after a while."

"I bet it does. I had to get out of the house. James and I fell out earlier."

Geraldine placed their cups on the kitchen table and invited her to take a seat. "Oh no. Why? You two are usually the most solid unmarried couple I know."

"Maybe it's time for us to reassess that tag."

Geraldine gasped. "There are two ways I could take that. Either you intend marrying him, which is the more unlikely scenario, given the expression on your face right now, or you're thinking about ending your relationship. Which is it?"

Ruth sighed and waved a hand in front of her. "When I figure that out, you'll be the first to know. It's been a hectic and frustrating day.

Enough about me. How are you feeling now? That's the most important question on my mind at present."

"Still feeling numb, I'll be honest with you, although I find myself having to put a brave face on when Mum and Dad are around."

"That's not right, sweetheart. You shouldn't have to conceal the truth about your feelings. It's an important part in the grieving process."

"I know; however, it gives me a far more peaceful life. I still can't believe I'll never see him again. I find myself sitting here, watching the back door, waiting for him to throw it open and take me into his arms. Soothe the pain away by telling me that it's all been a bad dream. I so want that to happen. Am I being plain ridiculous thinking that?"

Ruth placed a hand over her friend's. "I think you're acting like any normal grieving widow would in your position. I'm so sorry you're having to go through all this. You know I'm here for you, right?"

Geraldine gave her a tender smile. "I'd be lost if I didn't have you as a friend. Dare I ask how the investigation is going?"

"Sadly, not fast enough for my liking. I feel as though I'm letting you down when I have nothing significant to report."

"That's nonsense. Don't ever think that, Ruth, ever. You hear me?"

"I do. I've had an uber-frustrating day, chasing down some of the guests from the wedding. I called at Carmel Cove Hall to obtain the table plan to get all the names rather than bother you."

Geraldine tapped the side of her nose. "Now that's the type of thing Columbo would do."

Ruth sniggered. "I suppose watching all the Columbo episodes and Poirot films over the years has contributed greatly towards me and my business. It still takes a lot to sift through the clues to achieve the results, though."

"I can understand that. You're so thorough in everything you do, it was a no-brainer to employ your services. You know what the plod can be like at times."

"I know. Hopefully, between us, we'll soon be able to supply you with an answer as to who the culprit is soon. You'll need that to give you closure, allowing you to get on with your life."

"Do you think I'll ever get over losing Bradley? My heart is still aching painfully."

"Of course you will. It's only been a few days. Hang in there. We'll all be here to help you. You'll never be cast aside and left to grieve alone. Not unless that's the way you want things further down the line."

"Thank you. That truly means a lot. What happens next?"

Ruth shrugged. "I continue with the investigation. Ringing people to see if they either overheard Bradley talking to anyone or if someone saw a person venture up the stairs to the turret. I'm ringing the people who are further afield at the moment before I start questioning those who live in the town. I'd rather do that face to face if at all possible."

"Sounds like you have everything sussed out. Is there anything you need me to do?"

Ruth grinned sheepishly. "Answer a few questions when you're feeling more up to it."

"Hey, just opening up to you about how I feel has lessened the pain around my heart. Go on, ask me anything you like."

"If you're sure?" Geraldine nodded. "Okay, I need to ask you if Bradley had fallen out with anyone lately. Did he confide in you about things like that? Or keep that type of thing under wraps?"

Geraldine sipped at her cooled coffee. Replacing her cup on the table, she said, "I might need a few moments to think that over."

"Take all the time in the world. I'm in no rush to get back to the cottage and my non-blissful existence."

"You really are too harsh on James. He loves you to pieces. Anyone with half a brain could see that."

"Maybe."

Silence filled the room until Geraldine's eyes widened and she reached out to grip Ruth's hand. "His best friend, John Calshaw."

"What about him?" Ruth tried to cast her mind back to the

wedding. She didn't remember seeing John at the ceremony or the reception even.

"They fell out a few months ago."

"Do you know why?" Ruth asked.

"No. I've been sitting here trying to figure that out before I considered mentioning his name. I haven't got a clue."

"Was he at the wedding?"

"He wasn't invited. How do we know he didn't slip in unnoticed and do the deed?"

"Now who's being the amateur sleuth?"

"Ooo…there's a thought. Maybe we should team up and go into business together."

"You wouldn't give up your job of teaching the little ones, would you? All that training, plus the amount of holiday you teachers get during the year."

"It's a fallacy. We don't get that much time off. Most of it is spent planning out the next term's lessons. Maybe I should consider a change in career. Start afresh, somewhere new."

"No. You can't do that. I'd miss you for a start, and yes, that's me being totally selfish."

"Ignore me. I really don't know what to do for the best about the future. All I keep thinking about at the moment is what lies ahead of me with regard to the plans for the funeral. It sickens me that I should be sunning myself in the Caribbean with my new husband this week." Sadness descended, and tears swam in her eyes.

"I know, lovely. Hang in there. I can help with the arrangements if you want. You're not alone in this, you know that."

"I know. Maybe I'll be able to get my head around it more once the idea has settled. I've been told the pathologist won't release the body for at least a week anyway. So, there's no real rush."

"I forgot about that. Yes, they'll need to keep his body in case anything significant turns up during the investigation. Has Inspector Littlejohn been in touch with you?"

"She visited me briefly in the hospital. By then the doctors had given me medication, therefore I wasn't very lucid. Not sure how much sense I was making in answering her questions. She told me that she'd pay me a visit once I got home. I'm presuming she'll stop by soon."

"Thankfully, I've only bumped into her once. That was on the day of the...wedding," she said, correcting herself quickly when the first word that came into her head was *murder*.

"You hate each other. I hope that won't be a hindrance to your case."

"It won't. I promise to stay out of her way as much as possible. Right, I'd better go home, see if James has calmed down yet, that is unless you want me to hang around with you for a while longer?"

"No. You go and try to rectify things with James. Take my word that he does love you, everyone but you can see how much. Be kind to him. You'll only regret it if you break up. There's often no way back, lovely."

"Okay, pep talk taken on board. I'm going to shoot off. I'll pay John a visit tomorrow."

Geraldine walked Ruth and Ben out to the car and hugged Ruth after she'd settled Ben in the back. "Thank you for dropping by. Keep me up to date with things as they progress, if you will?"

"That goes without saying. Take care. Don't put up with any crap from your parents either. Tell them to tone their arguments down or take a hike."

Geraldine's head tilted to one side. "Why don't you listen to your own advice where James is concerned?"

"Whatever. I'm out of here. Love you lots."

Geraldine blew her a kiss. "Love you, too, my dearest friend."

When she entered the back door of her home, she heard the TV on in the living room. She pulled a white tea towel from the drawer and walked into the hallway. She waved the towel around the doorway of the lounge, and relief flooded through her when James laughed.

"Come in here, you silly woman."

She poked her head around the doorframe and smiled. "Are you still angry with me?"

"Are you with me?" he replied, still smiling broadly.

She ran and launched herself onto his lap. "I'm sorry. Can you ever forgive me?"

"I'm still thinking about that one. I will say one thing."

"What's that?"

"You're forgetting something, Ruth."

"I am?"

"We're both on the same side. I've never let you down in the past, have I?"

She dipped her head, ashamed of the way she'd spoken to him. "I know. I'm truly sorry."

"Where did you go?"

"I drove around for a while and then dropped by to see Geraldine. If anything, she's the one who pointed out the error of my ways." She cringed as she admitted that to him.

"Oh, did she now? You can be such an obstinate madam at times."

"I know. But it doesn't prevent you from loving me."

"Fortunately, it doesn't. I was just thinking about going up to bed. You could always join me for an early night."

Ruth smirked. "But I don't fancy reading tonight. I haven't got a good book on the go."

He raised his eyebrows and patted her on the backside. "Who said anything about reading?"

CHAPTER 8

RUTH MADE the decision to get on the road early the following morning. John Calshaw lived approximately twenty minutes away. She began her journey with Ben at seven-thirty, forgoing her breakfast. She'd make up for that by calling in at the baker's on her way to the office later.

She knocked on the front door of the terraced house in a quiet estate in Wayverley. A man opened the door, wearing a puzzled expression.

"Hello, John. Remember me? We've met a few times over the years at functions attended by Geraldine and Bradley."

"Ah, yes. Wait a minute, aren't you the private investigator?"

"Good memory. Do you mind if I come in and have a word with you?"

He glanced at his watch. "I'm due to leave for school in a few minutes. Can't this wait?"

"I'll be in and out, I promise."

He sighed and stepped behind the door, allowing her access to his hallway. He closed the door then instructed, "Follow me. I'll finish off my breakfast while we talk."

"Of course. First question is, can you tell me why you and Bradley fell out a few months ago?"

He frowned and took a bite of his toast which he chewed several times then swallowed. "Who told you that?"

"Geraldine."

"I'd rather not say at this point, not until you tell me why you're here."

"Geraldine has employed me to investigate who murdered Bradley."

"What? And you think I did it? Are you *mad*? Just because I fell out with my best friend, it doesn't mean that I would conjure up a bizarre way of killing him."

"Please, calm down. I'm simply asking a few questions to get some background, that's all."

He raked a hand through his short dark hair. "I'm sorry."

"I don't recall seeing you at the ceremony. Were you there?"

"No. Which is another reason why I couldn't have possibly killed him. I'm gutted he's dead. Are you a hundred percent sure he was murdered? Couldn't he have fallen off the turret by accident?"

Ruth inclined her head. "You really think that's plausible, John?"

"About as plausible as thinking that one of the guests at the wedding could be responsible for his death. Anyway, I was away with the local boys' football team. Bradley actually asked me to stand in for him, if you must know."

"I see. Where did you travel to? And what time was the match?"

"The coach picked us up from the town hall around twelve, and the match was on the other side of Bristol. It was a good ninety-minute trip there. The match was at three o'clock."

"Did you win?" Ruth smiled, trying to put the het up man at ease a little.

His head tilted one way and then the other. "No, it was a draw. Better than losing, though. I was shocked to hear the news when we returned that evening. Some of the boys were in tears."

"It's good to know the boys liked Bradley."

His gaze dropped to the kitchen table, and his hand twisted the mug.

"John, what aren't you telling me?"

His head rose, and his gaze connected with hers. "Some of the kids hated him. Hang on, that might be a little over the top. Let's say some of them disliked him."

A chill ran up her spine. "Why is that? I know pupils can't always like the teachers or coaches they work with, but what was the reason behind some of them not liking Bradley?"

His gazed dropped again. He swallowed noisily then said, "Because he was a bully."

Flabbergasted, and with the wind knocked out of her, Ruth fell back in the chair. "What? How in God's name does a coach bully his team?"

Still avoiding eye contact, he replied quietly, "It's the reason I fell out with him. Recently we'd made it up, only because he'd seen the error of his ways and swore that he was going to change."

"And had he?"

"It was too soon to know that. All I can tell you is that he appeared to be making an effort. Some of the boys had started to trust him again, others were proving impossible to get back onside."

"I don't think Geraldine was aware of this, was she?"

"I asked him that very question. He told me that he hadn't had the courage to tell her. As far as she knew, all the boys adored him."

"Oh heck, how am I supposed to tell her the opposite was true? What an absolute mess."

He glanced up at the clock on the kitchen wall. "I'm sorry, time's marching on, and I'm going to be late if I don't leave now."

Ruth smiled and stood. She offered him her hand to shake. "Thank you for seeing me and divulging what you have. At least now I have some kind of foundation to build on. Do you know if this bullying stretched to the kids at school as well as the football team?"

He shrugged into his jacket. "I really can't tell you that. Maybe if it did go that far it'll all come to light now that he's dead. Sorry, that sounded a bit severe."

"Not in the slightest. It sounded truthful. Thanks for taking the time to speak with me. I hope you make it to school in time and that the headmistress doesn't dish out a detention as punishment."

He smiled, his teeth gleaming under the bright kitchen light. "I don't think that's very likely. It was a pleasure speaking with you. Give me a shout if you think I can be of further help."

"That's very kind, thank you. I'll bear it in mind."

He collected his briefcase from the hallway and showed her to the front door.

Ruth sat in her car for a while, long after John had driven off. She contemplated whether Geraldine knew about the bullying and had chosen to ignore it or if she was oblivious to it all.

What if one of the parents attended the wedding and demanded to have a showdown up in the turret?

Was someone that furious that they were desperate to have it out with Bradley and overstepped the mark? Could there have been some form of altercation? Did a boy's father push him to teach him a lesson and went too far?

She sighed. How would she ever find out the answers now that Bradley was dead? Dead bodies couldn't speak, the last time she heard. She shuddered at the thought of having a conversation with a corpse down at the morgue. "That's not going to happen, Ben. Not while there's a breath left in my body."

Ben moaned and looked around him, probably wondering why she hadn't started the car yet. Thinking she only had one option left open to her, she got on the phone to the members of her club and asked if they could meet up at around twelve-thirty for lunch.

Ten minutes later, lunch was arranged. She would leave the office at twelve and stop off at the baker's for filled rolls and cakes. She had a rough idea of what each member of the group liked and didn't like in their rolls. She'd opt to get a mixture—you couldn't go wrong with a variety of fillings to feed the masses.

The rest of the morning consisted of her making yet more phone calls to the lesser known guests at the wedding, which involved asking the same tedious questions over and over and receiving the same answers in return. No one had either seen anyone talking to Bradley upstairs or had passed him on the staircase. It was all rather strange.

She decided to leave the office a little earlier than she'd originally intended to take Ben for a quick run at the park. Again, she fleetingly met Cynthia with her poodle. They had the briefest of chats before Ruth excused herself and Ben. After securing him in the back seat, she drove to the baker's to pick up lunch for the group.

Twenty pounds lighter in her purse, she strolled into the town hall and filled the kettle, then pulled a few chairs around one of the larger tables, ready for when the rest of the group arrived.

Hilary was the first to show up, followed swiftly by all the others. She felt proud that everyone had taken her call seriously and turned up for the impromptu meeting. With the initial hellos out of the way, everyone grabbed a roll of their choice and listened to what Ruth had to say.

"We love it when you involve us in an investigation," Hilary pointed out, smiling gleefully.

That smile didn't remain on her face for long once Ruth informed them about what she'd learned from John that morning.

"So, you're telling us that you think someone killed him because he was a bully?" Gemma asked, nibbling on her egg mayonnaise roll, ensuring the filling didn't ooze out of the sides.

"It seems likely. What I wanted to know is if any of you had ever witnessed any of that sort of behaviour from him or had heard anyone mentioning being affected by his callous bullying." She scanned the sea of faces, munching on their individual lunches, in expectation. It was then she noticed how fidgety Hilary had become all of a sudden. "Spit it out, Hils. I know when you're dying to get something out."

"Well, far be it for me to speak ill of the dead, but…"

"But you're going to." Gemma laughed.

Hilary glared at her. "All right, I'll keep my opinion to myself if nobody wants to hear what I have to say."

Gemma tutted. "It was a joke, Hils. Lighten up. Stop living on the edge of your nerves all day, every day."

Ruth slammed her hand on the table. It wasn't the first time she'd had to intervene once the two ladies started having a go at each other. "Gemma, Hils, come on. This is neither the time nor the place. I want to get on with this investigation for Geraldine's sake. Can you possibly put your differences aside for ten minutes?"

"Suits me. As I was saying before I was rudely interrupted," Hils continued, casting a second glare at Gemma, who had the foresight to remain tight-lipped this time round. "Well, Mrs Phillips brought one of her two lads into the surgery a few months ago. He was covered in bad bruises on his legs."

Ruth's ears pricked up. She urged Hilary to carry on; she had a tendency to pause mid-sentence for dramatic effect. "Go on, Hils, don't stop there."

"Well. Once the boy and his mother left the surgery, I was busy putting the patients' notes away when I might have overheard a conversation between two of the doctors. One of the doctors had seen the boy that morning and was unsure what to make of his injuries. The other one said that he should contact Social Services if he had concerns."

"Really? They were that bad? You don't think it was possible the mother might have caused them and was keen to apportion the blame elsewhere?"

Some of the group laughed.

"Only a PI would think along those lines, Ruth, come off it," Lynn piped up.

Ruth cringed. "Sorry. Welcome to my world, everyone. I'm so suspicious of people nine-tenths of the time."

"Don't think that snippet of information has gone unnoticed in the past," Lynn replied with a cheeky smile.

"Okay. Hils, getting back to what you overheard, did the boy say where he'd got these bruises?"

"From playing football."

Ruth groaned. "Highly probable, isn't it?"

"Well, my nephew plays in his school's football team, and he's never once complained about being kicked around," Lynn suggested.

"Exactly," Hils replied. "It's not that common, Ruth. In my eyes it would be worth going further, maybe call round to question the lad or his mother to get the ins and outs of what actually went on. They're sure to tell the truth now there's no recourse to their actions. Anyway, the mother confided in me, while she was sitting in the waiting room with the lad that she'd had suspicions about the coach for a while. That's why she forced her son to go to the doctor. That way they'd have something definitive on record, should the need arise later on."

"Wow, do parents go that extra mile for their kids nowadays?" The words were out before Ruth had a chance to rein them in. With plenty of parents in the group, she braced herself for an onslaught.

"Hey, most parents care what happens to their kids. It's not fair of you to tar all parents with the same brush," Lynn replied, her back stiffening as she spoke.

"I'm sorry, it came out wrong. My mistake." She turned back to Hilary and asked, "Hils, do you know what came of the incident in the end?"

"I was interested so chased it up myself and looked through the boy's records. The bruising eventually died down, and no charges were brought against Bradley by SS because the boy refused to blame his coach."

Ruth gasped. "No, do you think he got to the boy? Threatened him to keep quiet, or even bribed him?"

Hilary shrugged. "Your guess is as good as mine. I know what I would do if I were in your shoes, seeking answers."

Ruth leaned forward, her eyes wide with expectation. "What's that?"

"Well, I'd break down the headmistress's door and demand to be heard."

Ruth smiled and relaxed her frame. "I'll make PIs of you lot yet. That, my dear lady, is exactly what I intend doing. This afternoon, in fact."

"Good for you. Maybe this is the key that will unlock the secret chest to the mystery," Steven added, in his own theatrical way.

They chatted generally after that, mainly voicing their concerns about Geraldine, shocked that she'd been in hospital over the weekend but glad that she'd made a full recovery. After they'd completed their lunch, they parted company, promising to get together in a few days if everyone was available to begin creating the costumes for the show, which was creeping up on them and only a few weeks ahead. Steven was already in a spin about it and moaning that his sleep pattern had been affected drastically due to his mind constantly being on the go.

RUTH DROVE TO HIGHGATE SCHOOL. Fortunately, the headmistress was free to see her but made it clear that she could only spare ten minutes for the interview.

"Thank you, Miss Scott. I know how valuable your time is. I'll come straight to the point in that case. As you're probably aware, Bradley Sinclair lost his life at the weekend."

Miss Scott nodded, a sad expression descending on her wrinkle-free face. "I heard. On his wedding day, too, of all times."

"That's right. Well, Geraldine, his new wife, has asked me to delve into the tragic incident."

"You? Why you? Why not leave the investigation in the capable hands of the police?"

"Because she knows that I have had excellent results over the years in my role as a PI. Have the police visited you yet?"

"No, they haven't. Why would they?"

"I rest my case. I would've thought visiting a victim's place of work would be at the very top of their agenda. I know the inspector running the investigation, and, well, I'm not convinced that she conducts her investigations with the vigour that is expected of her. Maybe she'll up her game on this one and prove me wrong, or maybe that's wishful thinking on my part."

"If you have an axe to grind with the inspector, that's your prerogative, Miss Morgan."

"I'm willing to set it aside. I assure you, she's the one not playing ball. Talking of which, I have a few questions I'd like to ask you about Bradley, if you don't mind?"

"Fire away. Like I said at the beginning of this meeting, I can only spare you a few minutes, so use the time wisely."

"I will. Okay, it's come to light this morning, while I was interviewing someone else connected with this crime, that Bradley was, how shall I put this? Overzealous in the way he handled the pupils under his care."

Miss Scott's brow wrinkled. "In what way?" she asked, linking her hands in front of her on the desk.

"I've heard on the grapevine that he used to bully the boys on the football team he coached. It would seem logical to me to ask if he'd been found guilty of doing the same to the pupils at this school."

"Firstly, no, I have never heard of such rumours, and secondly, there are rules in place at this school protecting the pupils, and the staff for that matter, against bullying. I would never have tolerated such behaviour," Miss Scott replied stiffly.

"I'm glad to hear it. Perhaps you've overheard Bradley falling out with another member of staff?"

"No. Nothing of that ilk at all. Are you suggesting that one of the teachers went to the wedding with the intention of harming Bradley?"

"Not specifically, but it's not something I should discount either, as I'm sure you agree."

"I can understand that. Although, I have to stick up for my staff on this one. I don't have anyone working in this school who possesses such a vile temper to possibly do such a thing."

"Was he well liked amongst the staff?"

"Extremely I would say, which is why you casting aspersions is upsetting me."

Ruth smiled tightly. "I'm sorry. All I'm doing is trying to get to the bottom of why my best friend became a wife and a widow within the space of an hour on Saturday. If I upset or step on anyone's toes during my interviews, then I'm afraid that can't be helped. Geraldine has a right to know who killed the man she loved."

"I'm not disputing that, Miss Morgan. Does your friend know that you're putting it around that he was a bully? If not, my suggestion would be that you put that right immediately if she doesn't."

"I will be ringing her soon, to give her an update. I'll be sure to give her all the information that has come my way throughout the day." Ruth had a sinking feeling that she was getting nowhere fast. *Maybe Bradley didn't bully the kids at school, only on his football team.* She hoped that was right. Surely if it wasn't, the kids wouldn't have put up with his bullying without plastering it all over social media. Wasn't that what kids did nowadays? Which to Ruth's mind was in itself a form of bullying. The world had gone nuts in that respect.

"I have to go now. Was there anything else you wanted to ask, Miss Morgan?" Miss Scott stood and walked around the desk, ready to show Ruth out.

"No. That's all for now. Would it be okay to revisit you if I think of anything else?"

"Maybe we could discuss anything further over the phone instead. My working day is hectic most days."

"I understand. Once again, I thank you for sparing the time to see me in your busy schedule." Ruth held her hand out.

Miss Scott shook it, her wrist as limp as a rotten cabbage leaf. Ruth's father had warned her about people with limp handshakes: people who insisted on using them were often insincere. She returned to the car, wondering if Miss Scott was insincere or if the myth was a load of codswallop.

She stopped off to give Ben a run along the coastal path and then made her way home. She was almost there when she spotted the ambulance sitting outside her sister's house. "Oh no!" Yanking on the handbrake, she darted out of the car and into the house.

"Carolyn, what's going on?"

Her sister rushed into her arms, tears cascading down her face as two paramedics tended to a very pale-looking Keith. Ruth's gaze drifted to his hand. Blood was seeping through the towel wrapped around it. It appeared to be serious.

"He was using a circular saw, and it slipped," Carolyn told her in between sobs.

"He'll be all right, hon. They'll take him to hospital and get him stitched up."

"I think he'll need more than stitching," Carolyn replied quietly, as if saying the words aloud would make the situation a whole lot worse.

"I'll come with you. Give me five minutes to drop Ben home, and I'll be back, all right? Don't go into a meltdown, I know you."

"I won't. Don't be long."

Keith wailed when the paramedics removed the towel and the blood arced across the room.

Ruth's stomach lurched. "I'll be back soon." She kissed her sister and ran back to the car. After unhooking Ben from his harness, she whisked him along the road and let herself into the house. She then hurriedly scribbled a note to James, explaining the situation, and left the house again.

Five minutes later, the ambulance was on its way to the hospital with Carolyn and Ruth in hot pursuit. "What about the kids?"

Carolyn waved her apprehension away. "I asked Mrs Lake to watch out for them. She said she'd give them their tea, bless her. I love it when the neighbours come to our aid. What would we do without them? She heard me scream. If it hadn't been for her ringing the ambulance, I would still be standing there in shock, staring at Keith."

"She's a sweetie. Please, you mustn't worry about Keith. He's in safe hands now."

"What if he loses it?"

"What? His hand? Was it really that bad?"

Out of the corner of her eye she saw Carolyn turn to face her. "You saw how much blood there was. I reckon he's lost a couple of pints already. Oh gosh, I think I'm going to be sick." Her sister retched.

Ruth indicated and pulled up at the side of the road. She reached across Carolyn and flung the door open. "Not in my car you don't."

Carolyn leaned over and emptied her stomach in the gutter. In the distance, the ambulance was getting further and further away from them. Ruth extracted a tissue from a box she kept in the centre console and handed it to her sister.

"Better?"

"Hardly. How do you define better when your throat has just been burned by acid?"

"You get my drift. Come on, shut the door, we need to get on the road again."

Ruth pressed her foot down on the accelerator, her aim to catch up with the ambulance ahead. All she succeeded in doing was making Carolyn feel sicker than she already was. Carolyn held one hand over her mouth and tugged at Ruth's sleeve with the other. Right about then she mentally kicked herself for not having a sick bag tucked away in her glove compartment.

"Hang on, we're almost there now. Can you do that?"

Carolyn pulled open the door, forcing Ruth to slam on the brakes while she barfed.

Another couple of minutes passed before they were able to get on the road again. The rest of the journey, thankfully, was vomit-free. Ruth parked the car and the pair of them ran through the main entrance. Spotting the signs for Accident and Emergency, Ruth grabbed Carolyn's arm and bolted down the corridor, following the colour-coded line that would lead them to their destination.

"I can't keep up with you," Carolyn complained, lagging behind.

"Come on. We're almost there now."

Within seconds, they had reached the department. The receptionist told them to take a seat in the family waiting room, adding that a doctor would be out to see them as soon as he or she was free. Carolyn flopped into a chair and placed her head in her hands. It had been a whirlwind twenty minutes. Ruth realised she would need to call on all her resources to be strong enough for them both. She sought out two cups of water and handed one to Carolyn.

"Here, drink this, it'll make you feel better."

"Thanks, I'd rather have a cup full of brandy, though."

Ruth smiled. "It's good to see you've still got your sense of humour. He'll be fine, you'll see."

"But how can he be, when he's lost so much blood?" Carolyn downed the rest of her water and placed the empty cup on the small table beside her.

"Thinking negatively isn't going to help. Try and spin that on its head and think positively. I appreciate how hard that's going to be, but Keith is going to need to see you coping better than you are about this."

"I could seriously do without one of your know-it-all lectures right now, sis."

Ruth held her arms out to the sides and let them slap against her thighs. "I'm not lecturing you. All I'm trying to do is ease the tension and ask you to think about things practically. Knowing how Keith's mind works, he's probably in there, worrying that he's letting you and the kids down rather than about the injuries he has. He's promised you all you'd be in the newly renovated house by Christmas. The likelihood of that happening now will be playing on his mind. You're going to need to get across to him that his health is more important than keeping a promise."

"Why thank you, ma'am. What would I do without your insight into my relationship?" Carolyn snapped back, her words laced with sarcasm.

Ruth flew across the room and sank into the chair beside her, gathered her sister's hands in her own and looked her straight in the eye. "You know me, love, I shoot from the hip. I didn't mean it to come out sounding that harsh, I'm sorry."

"I know. I didn't mean to bite back either. What are we like?"

The conversation came to an abrupt halt when a young man wearing blue scrubs entered the room. "Mrs Everett?"

Carolyn jumped out of her seat. Ruth did the same and placed an arm around her waist, ready to support her sister if her legs gave way.

"That's me. How is he?"

"He's lost a lot of blood, I think you realise that. He's lucky the ambulance reached him when it did. He's going to need an operation. You're aware he cut two of his fingers off?"

Carolyn swooned; Ruth held her upright.

"Can you stick them back on?" Ruth asked, forgetting what the correct terminology should be in instances like this.

The doctor grinned. "Yes, we have the fingers. They will be

stitched in place again. He's going to need months of recuperation before he'll be able to use them properly again."

"But we're renovating the house and were hoping to be in before Christmas," Carolyn whined.

The doctor shook his head slowly. "If you're doing the renovations yourselves, then things will have to be put on hold."

"We are. Oh my, what on earth are we going to do now?"

Ruth squeezed her sister tightly. "We'll all muck in and help. The community will pull together." She knew she was wrong voicing her hopes but she also knew how important it was to keep her sister's spirits high. *Gosh, as if I haven't got enough on my plate already with the investigation. Now I'm going to have to make good on my word and rally people in the community to lend a hand.*

"I hope you're right, Ruth. We could do with the extra help."

Ruth nodded. "Let's discuss the finer details later. Doc, will Keith be in hospital long?"

"It depends how the surgery goes. I think you should expect him to be with us for around a week."

"Thank you. That'll give us a chance to get things organised at home. There's nothing for it, Carolyn, you're all going to have to move in with me and James."

Her sister let out a long, relieved sigh. "That would be fantastic. Thank you."

"Right. I must get on. Do you ladies want to see him before he goes down for surgery?"

"Yes, that would be lovely, thank you, Doctor," Carolyn replied, anxiously gripping Ruth's hand.

"Come with me." He led them down the corridor to a small room where they found Keith lying in bed.

Carolyn rushed towards him, sobbing, and flung her arms around his neck. Keith seemed a little out of it, doped up to the eyeballs on medication ready for his operation.

"Hello, mate, how's it going?" Ruth asked, rubbing his upper arm.

"Stupid, ain't I? Not sure what made me start to use the thing with the cable in the way. I tried to move it, and that's when I slipped on some debris underfoot. You know what? For a few seconds I didn't even realise what I'd done. There was no pain. Realised soon enough when I saw my two fingers lying on the floor beneath me."

Ruth nodded. "It must have been a huge shock. You're going to be all right, Keith. You're in expert hands. Don't worry about a thing."

"I'm worried about all the work ahead of me. I can't possibly do that with only one hand."

"Right, I'm going to leave you guys to discuss things. We'll be taking you down in five minutes. Try not to fight the medication, Mr Everett," the doctor advised before he left the room.

Ruth smiled at Keith. "You heard what the doc said, we'll discuss this later, Keith. You need to relax and let the medication take over."

He leaned back against the pillow. His eyelids started drooping as they watched him relax. Moments later, a hospital porter arrived to take him down to the operating theatre.

"I'll be here when you wake up. Good luck," Carolyn called after him.

"Come on. I'll take you to the restaurant, buy you a coffee and a sandwich, something to keep your strength up." Ruth had to point her sister in the right direction; her gaze was still drawn to the porter pushing the bed up the corridor. It wasn't until they'd gone through the door at the end that Carolyn's attention turned back to her once more.

They walked off in the opposite direction.

Once they'd located the small restaurant, neither of them was hungry. Ruth bought them both a coffee and a chocolate muffin they could share. They found a seat by the window, overlooking the vast parking lot which had a view of the hillside beyond.

"Do you really think we'll be able to rally people to help us? It seems a bit of a cheek. If only we could afford to pay a building firm to take over the work. That would take the pressure off a little."

"That's it. Instead of begging people to lend a hand in the community, we'll organise a Go Fund Me through the internet."

Carolyn shuddered at the thought. "Isn't that like putting out a begging bowl for people to drop a few pennies in that they've found down the back of the couch?"

Ruth wrinkled her nose. "Don't be daft. Some of these funds raise thousands of pounds for the right cause. Let me think about how to word a campaign this evening. There's no guarantee it'll work, though, so don't come down heavy on me if it goes tits up."

"He, he, I've always loved that expression. You have my word on that. Thanks, Ruth, you always think of a solution to a problem."

"I'm always here for you. I meant what I said about moving into the house, too."

"Shouldn't you run that past James first?"

"Leave him to me. He'll be putty in my hands."

"If you say so. I won't be offended if you retract the offer once you run it past James and he thinks the idea sucks. Anyway, I think we'll be fine for a few months, while the good weather is still with us."

"We'll cross that bridge when we come to it then. I hope the surgery goes well. It's amazing what they can do nowadays, right?"

"I shudder at the thought of him being unable to use his hands properly, what with him being an electrician. That reminds me, I'm going to have to get on to the insurance people when I get home."

"Will they cover him? Seeing the incident was an accident that happened in his own home and not while he was on the job, so to speak?"

Carolyn gasped and covered her mouth. "Crumbs, I never thought of that. Whatever will we do?"

"Not worry would be my first suggestion. I'll add that information to the campaign I'll set up. It's bound to pull at people's heartstrings more, especially if Keith is self-employed with a family he needs to feed."

Carolyn closed her eyes and held her crossed fingers up in the air. "I do hope you're right."

SEVERAL HOURS LATER, after they'd both worn out a patch in the waiting room floor with their pacing, a nurse came to collect them to take them up to the men's ward. Keith was still unconscious, his injured arm raised up in a pully. Ruth settled Carolyn next to her husband and then excused herself. She'd promised her sister she would collect her two sons from the neighbour and feed them, if Mrs Lake hadn't already done it.

Ian and Robin were both understandably worried about their father and were exceptionally quiet while Ruth prepared the dinner. She'd expected them to bombard her with questions, of the gory variety, but they didn't.

James came home looking confused. He pecked Ruth on the cheek and motioned with his head towards the boys who were playing Tetris or some such game on their phones. "What's going on?"

"We're babysitting them for the evening. Keith is in hospital, and Carolyn is by his bedside. Is that a problem?"

"No. Wow, why's Keith in hospital? What's he done?"

"Sliced a couple of fingers off. He's had surgery now, but I had to jump in to help. Here, lay the table for me. I found some fish fingers in the freezer. I know you'd buried them for yourself. I'll buy you some more when I go shopping."

"There's no need. Was there enough for all of us?"

"For you three, yes. I'm not really hungry, too concerned about Keith and Geraldine to eat. I found out something interesting about Bradley today, something that could turn the case on its head. I'll tell you about that later."

"Sounds intriguing. Don't I even get a hint?"

"Nope. I'm too busy making sure I don't burn these chips and fish fingers."

James laughed and withdrew the cutlery from the drawer. The boys offered to lend a hand, too, and filled four glasses with orange juice and placed them on the table. Ruth smiled at her nephews' ability not to dwell on what was going on with their father.

Once the meal had ended, she suggested the boys go through to the living room to watch some TV while she and James cleared up the kitchen.

"Are you still in a mood with me?" he whispered in her ear.

"No. I have bigger fish to fry, excuse the pun. I'm sorry for falling out with you. We need to have a serious chat."

He frowned. "Sounds ominous. Is this chat about us?"

"In a roundabout way it is. Take a seat." She took the coffees she'd made over to the table and sat next to him. Lowering her voice so the boys couldn't hear, she revealed her plans.

"What? They're moving in?"

"Shh...keep it down. Not yet, when the weather gets bad. You wouldn't begrudge them having a dry roof over their heads, would you? They're no bother."

"I know. All right. You've talked me round."

She leaned over and kissed him to show her appreciation. "I'm also going to sit down tonight and start a Go Fund Me campaign."

"Now that's an excellent idea and one that I'm willing to get behind if you'll let me help you organise it."

"I was hoping you'd say that. We'll get that started in a few minutes."

"Done. Now, what's going on with the investigation?"

"You first?"

He shrugged. "Nothing from what I can tell. You said you'd discovered something today that you think will help."

"What exactly is Inspector Littlejohn doing during the day? As far as I can tell, she hasn't even started questioning the guests who attended the wedding yet. All right, she questioned a few of us on the day, but damn, there were over a hundred guests there."

"She's doing other things. I don't want to start slating her off to you when I'm not privy to what she and her team are up to. Are you going to tell me what you've learned?"

"I visited Bradley's ex-best friend this morning and, although they'd made it up again recently, he told me something shocking."

"I know how much you like to string these things out, but is there any chance you can get on with it? You know, I'm back on shift at six in the morning," he added with a smirk.

"Well, here's the thing. He was a bully. He used to bully the kids on the local football team."

"Wow, really? But he was a teacher, wasn't he?"

"Yes. Therefore, after I'd spoken to John Calshaw, his best friend, I immediately went to the school to seek the opinion of the head-mistress—who I have to say was absolutely appalled by the revelation."

James tapped the table with his fingers. "Interesting. So she doesn't think he was showing any signs of being a bully in the classroom then? Or do you think she wasn't aware and that possibly bullying *was* going on there?"

"I don't know. If I was a betting girl, maybe I'd be inclined to think the latter, that he disguised it well and that the headmistress was oblivious to what was going on."

"Holy cow!"

Ruth held a finger up, preventing him from saying anything further. "That's not all. I called an emergency meeting of the Am-Dram club and asked them if they'd ever heard or suspected Bradley of being a bully, when Hilary raised her hand to say yes, she'd heard something."

"Really? Oh wait, Hilary works as a receptionist at the doctor's surgery, right? Sorry to be so vague, I can never keep up with your group."

She nodded. "That's right, you're spot on."

"Isn't her role supposed to be confidential?"

"Yes, but there has to be an exception to the rule when it's a murder investigation, surely?"

He rolled his eyes and grinned. "Even if Bradley wasn't dead, you'd still wrangle the information out of people, wouldn't you?"

She chuckled. "You know me so well. Anyway, are you going to let me tell you what she said?" She stood and closed the kitchen door so the boys couldn't hear them. Then she returned to her seat. "One of the boys on the football team turned up at the surgery sporting a lot of bruises. His mother was very concerned and suspected her son was being abused, despite the fact that he denied it. She wanted the bruises noted down on his medical records for future reference."

"Seems like a logical idea. Great thinking by the mum, I'd say."

"Anyway, Hilary overheard two of the doctors talking, one of them seeking advice from the other one on what to do for the best."

"Social Services would need to be informed right away, wouldn't they?"

"That was the suggestion from the doctor offering the advice. My concern is that if he was playing football, how likely was it that Social Services were going to take action in an incident such as that?"

"I get your drift. Highly unlikely, which is such a shame. Maybe that was the thought behind the boy's reluctance to say anything."

"I think you're right. Here's my train of thought on this: what if he wasn't the only one? What if dozens of kids complained, or rather *didn't* complain, to their parents and it caused problems at home and—?"

"One of the parents took umbrage at the wedding and decided to take matters into their own hands?"

"Exactly. Think about it… Hypothetically, if you had a son and he was acting weird after every football session he attended but refused to speak to you about what was going on in his head, it wouldn't take you long to put two and two together. I'm thinking that if one of the parents was at the wedding—let's face it, most of the townsfolk were there, right? What if one of the fathers was churning up inside, knowing how broken his child was, seeing Bradley parading around with a huge smile on his face? Yes, it was his wedding day, but come on, wouldn't that tick you off? I know it would me."

"That seems a little far-fetched to me."

"Really? I think I've nailed it. Now all I have to do is start questioning people who attended the wedding and whose sons play on the football team."

"Good luck with that one. What about the best friend? Did he attend the wedding?"

Ruth shook her head. "Sadly not. He was away with the team on the day. He seemed pretty cut up about Bradley's death."

"I don't envy you trying to figure out the killer on this one, sweetie. There could be numerous suspects, especially if his bullying was rife."

"I know. That's the frustrating part. There were over one hundred attendees at that damn wedding. I know for a fact who it wasn't, you or me, but I can't vouch for any of the others."

"What? Surely you're not going to count Geraldine as a suspect, are you?"

"Sorry, I should have added her name along with ours. Gosh, what a tough investigation this is turning out to be, and it's only just begun. I could do with a helping hand from Littlejohn, but she seems to be taking her time, as usual. Remind me how she got to be an inspector again?"

"Rumour has it that she slept with a senior officer, but that's totally off the record."

"Why am I not surprised to hear that?"

"It is what it is. Have you told Geraldine about the bullying?"

"Not yet. I was going to drop by this evening but was waylaid by what happened to Keith. My priorities need to be with the boys tonight; they must be confused about what's going on with their father. Come on, enough chat, let's see if we can boost their spirits by having a game of Mario Kart, what do you say?"

James pushed back his chair and opened his arms. She stepped into them. "You're a good woman, Ruth Morgan, even if you do fly off the handle for no reason sometimes. I still love you."

Tears pricked her eyes. "I love you, too, James. Just remember that when I'm turning down another wedding proposal. It's me, nothing to do with you."

"I dispute that. It has everything to do with me, as I'm doing the proposing and getting shafted every time, but I forgive you."

"Good. Keep asking. One day I might surprise you and say yes, although not too soon after what happened over the weekend. Having a murder at a wedding is the pits and not something I'd like to repeat at ours...should that ever come about," she added quickly.

His response was to give her a long kiss that melted her heart. They walked into the living room. The boys were sitting on the couch, looking very subdued.

"Fancy a game of Mario Kart, boys?"

Their eyes lit up, and they sat forward in their seats. "Yes, please."

"Okay. Uncle James will set it up while I organise some nibbles for later because once I get started, I'm going to wipe the floor with you lot."

James motioned with his head towards Ruth. "Girls, eh?"

Ian and Robin laughed raucously. Ruth wandered back into the kitchen, grinning. They were good kids. She would do everything in her power to ensure their minds were taken off their recent troubles. Family was everything to her. She sourced the bowls and the savoury snacks she kept at the back of the larder cupboard out of James' reach —he was a devil for munching his way through the shopping every week. By the time she had placed all the contents on a tray and walked back into the living room, the game had been set up and the three of them were waiting impatiently for her to join them.

"Come on, slow coach, we've been ready for ten minutes," Ian, the younger of the two boys shouted, an exceptionally wide grin on his face.

"I'll just take this lot back into the kitchen then, shall I?"

"*No!*" they all shouted in unison.

Ruth laughed and placed the tray on the coffee table and picked up one of the four controllers. "Let the race begin. Stand aside, you guys, let the winner strut her stuff."

"Umm…how can you call yourself a winner when the races haven't even begun yet?" James asked.

"I'm simply going by our previous experiences, dear. Here we go!" she screeched, ramping up the excitement in the room.

The next few hours consisted of lots of noise and bouts of groaning when she finally lifted the winner's trophy—again. James presented the cutout trophy made of rigid card, and Ruth ran around the room singing, "I am the champion!" much to the boys' amusement in spite of their disappointment at losing.

"You're nuts, Auntie Ruth," Robin grumbled.

She placed the trophy on the mantelpiece and swooped in for a hug with her nephews. "I might be nuts, but you guys love me all the same, right?" The two boys tried to wriggle out of her grasp. She kissed them both on the cheeks and said, "Time for bed. Do you need anything before you go up?"

"Apart from a rematch because you cheated?" Robin muttered grumpily before he broke into a smile.

"Cheeky. It was a fun night, guys, even if I did wipe the floor with you."

The boys groaned and headed up the stairs to the spare room. Ruth had already placed a number of essential items on their beds, such as spare toothbrushes and toothpaste and a set of PJs she kept for emergencies, although, knowing her luck, they'd probably grown out of them by now.

Once he'd put the equipment away, James slipped an arm around her shoulder. "You're a fabulous aunt."

She cringed, knowing what was probably about to come next. "I love them to pieces. Right, I'd better see if I can get hold of Carolyn. I promised her I'd ring this evening before we went to bed. She'll want to know how the boys are."

"I'll put the kettle on and make us a coffee. All the shouting has made me hoarse."

Ruth grinned and picked up her phone. Her sister answered the call within a few seconds. "Hi, how's he doing?"

"He's fine. He woke up for a little while, complained that he was in pain, and they knocked him out with medication again. How are the boys?"

"Smarting because I won the trophy in Mario Kart. Apart from that they're fine, don't worry about them. Are you coming home soon?"

"No. I thought I'd stay here with him, do you mind?"

"Of course not. The boys have gone to bed. I'll give them their breakfast and take them to school in the morning."

"I don't know what I'd do without you, Ruth. I'll come home in the morning if Keith's all right. Thanks for being a wonderful sister."

"Right backatcha. You'd do the same for me if ever I was in dire straits."

"Probably. Goodnight, sweetheart."

"Sleep well. Don't worry about the boys, they're fine."

"Thank you."

Ruth ended the call then nipped around to her sister's caravan to get the boys a change of clothes for the morning, just so they weren't all running around like headless chickens. Then she and James sat down to enjoy their coffee.

"Fancy watching a film?"

Ruth shook her head. "I'm beat. It takes a lot of stamina for a *girl* to beat you boys. Think I'll go up for a read, or to plan out a to-do list of what I'll need to do tomorrow."

"Okay, I'll be up soon. There's a comedy I've had my eye on, not something that will appeal to you."

"Enjoy." She leaned over, kissed him and went to bed.

Her mind whirling regarding the case, she fell asleep about an hour later. Her final thought was whether she should visit Geraldine to make her aware of what Bradley had been up to. Was it too soon to tell her that information, though? How would she react?

CHAPTER 9

THE FOLLOWING morning was hectic from the word go, making her wonder how her sister coped with getting the boys ready for school, looking after the house—or caravan as it was—and getting involved in the renovations at the cottage. It wasn't until she was sitting behind her desk at gone nine that she realised she had neglected to plan out the Go Fund Me campaign. She made that a priority. Within half an hour, she'd set up the campaign and had texted the link to James for his approval. He replied to say it looked fantastic and that he'd make sure he put a poster up about it in the police canteen at lunchtime.

Every little would help. She smiled at her achievement then set her personal business aside to get back to the investigation. She continued the mundane task of working her way through the list of wedding guests, infuriated that no new leads came from any of the calls.

Around eleven, she decided it was time to make herself a coffee. She'd not long settled back in her chair when the phone rang. "Hello, Carmel Cove Detective Agency, Ruth speaking, how can I help you?"

There was a moment's silence until a muffled, gravelly voice said, "There's more to this crime than meets the eye."

"Sorry? What crime?"

"The one you're investigating."

Ruth frowned and then sat forward in her chair when her interest was piqued. "Are you talking about the Bradley Sinclair murder?"

"Bravo! Finally, the penny has dropped."

"What do you mean there's more to this crime than meets the eye? What do you know?"

"Dig deep to uncover the truth you seek."

She was about to ask what the person meant by that cryptic clue when they hung up. She searched the data in her phone—the call had come from an unregistered number. *Oh great, whoop-de-do!*

She was numb for several seconds. Her mind felt like a tornado had taken up residence in her head. Who could the caller be? *Am I on the right lines thinking it could be a parent of one of the football team? Or am I missing the mark completely?* She threw the pen across the other side of the room, missing Ben by inches. Wrapped in guilt, she shot out of her chair and hugged her four-legged companion. "I'm sorry, mate. Mummy shouldn't have lost her temper like that."

He moaned softly and licked her face, indicating all was forgiven. She gave him a treat and returned to her desk. An idea sparked in her mind, and she picked up the phone. "Hey, Louise, how are things going? Sorry, it's Ruth here."

Louise worked as a reporter on the local paper, *The Carmel Cove Times*. "Hi, Ruth, how are things with you?"

"Do you have five minutes to have a chat?"

"On the phone or in person?"

"It would be great to see you face to face. Do you have the time?"

"What about the Cove Coffee shop in, say, half an hour?"

"That would be ideal. See you then, Louise." Ruth ended the call and gathered the pieces of evidence she'd so far uncovered about the case. She trusted Louise with her life. They'd been friends since their days at school, and she'd never let her down in the past.

Fetching Ben's leash, she locked up the office and took him for a run at the park in town before she headed to the coffee shop for her meeting.

Ruth insisted the drinks were on her when Louise arrived.

"Thanks so much for coming. I had a perplexing call come in this morning and I don't mind telling you, it's put me in a spin."

"Whoa, hang on a second, let me have a sip of coffee and take down some notes."

Ruth cringed. "Do you have to? I really don't want this getting out in the open just yet."

Louise frowned. "Are you saying you don't trust me?"

"You know I'm not saying that. Okay, make your notes. Right, you know what happened at the wedding at the weekend. That news shouldn't come as a shock to you."

"Yep, it was appalling. What makes the police think it's murder?" Louise took another sip of her latte.

Looking around her to ensure no one could overhear their conversation, Ruth leaned in and said, "I'm not really privy to that information. They wouldn't let me near the scene, and the inspector and I don't really get on. My take is that her way of thinking is: why would the groom kill himself when he walked down the aisle only an hour or so before?"

"There's a certain amount of logic to that. So, what's your problem?"

"My problem is, that I've since found out that Bradley—and this remains between you and me for now at least, okay?"

"Yes, I swear on my grandfather's grave. Go on, what have you uncovered? Was he cheating on Geraldine?"

"No, it was nothing like that. I've since discovered that he was a bully. He coached the local football team. Or rather bullied them into playing for him."

"Wow, that's insane. Who told you this?"

"A reliable source, his best friend. Actually, he fell out with him over this issue."

"Crikey. Where has that led you in the investigation?"

"I have another source who told me a concerned mother took her son to the doctor with mysterious bruises after he had attended a football match under Bradley's supervision."

"I don't understand. Isn't that a given, that the boys would end up with bruises during training or a game?"

"Not according to some other parents I've spoken to whose kids play for another team."

"Hmm…in that case, maybe you're right to be concerned."

Ruth raised a finger. "That's not all. I was going through the list of wedding attendees at the office this morning, ringing a few of them to see if they'd witnessed anything untoward at the reception, when my phone rang. I answered it and was confronted with someone obviously doing their best to disguise their voice."

"Interesting. Are you going to tell me what they said?"

"I will if you have some patience. The person told me that I needed to dig deep and that there was more to the murder than met the eye."

"Is that it?"

"Yes. Bizarre, right?"

"Totally. Are you sure it's not a nutjob, trying to lead you down a wrong path?"

Ruth shrugged. "That's a possibility. What do you think I should do about it?"

Louise held her arms out to the sides. "How should I know?"

"Oh gosh, I thought you'd be able to help me."

"Not with the phone call. How about I do some digging on Bradley, will that suffice?"

Ruth's dejected spirit rose. "Would you? That would be cool. I need to get cracking with questioning the other guests. I'm only about a quarter of the way through the list. It's been a nightmare so far, what with one thing or another. Two people who I love dearly have ended up in hospital in the past few days, and that has put the investigation behind."

"Two people? I heard about Geraldine on the grapevine, but who's the other one?"

"My brother-in-law. He sliced two fingers off whilst carrying out renovations on their house. He had an operation yesterday. I had to be there with Carolyn; she needed my support."

Louise shuddered and shook her head. "Ugh, that's dreadful. The operation, was that to repair the damage?"

"No, they've managed to stitch the fingers back on. It's jeopardised their plans to have the renos completed by Christmas, though. Enough about our problems. If you can do some digging and get back to me ASAP, you know how appreciated I'd be."

"I do. Where would you be without me at times, eh?"

"Exactly. It works both ways. I've given you a few decent headlines over the years, too, remember?"

"I do. I'd better be off before the boss gets antsy. Lovely to see you, I'll be in touch soon."

"Thanks, Louise. Can you keep things under wraps for now?"

"Until you give me the go-ahead."

Louise hugged her and left the coffee shop. Ruth finished off her own coffee at leisure, going over certain aspects of the case that were bugging her. She withdrew her phone and swiped through the photos she had taken on the day. Zooming in to them highlighted something unnerving that she had previously missed.

Now she was faced with yet another dilemma: should she visit Geraldine, tell her about the mysterious phone call and what she'd uncovered so far? Or did she take an alternative route now that the investigation had spun off in a different direction?

She flipped through a dozen or so more photos and spotted yet another clue that she had missed. She kicked herself under the table, downed the rest of her coffee and rushed back to the car. Needing to clear her head a little, she drew up at the park and let Ben out again. As he ran after a few of the squirrels darting from tree to tree, her mind was whisked up into a frenzy. She soon came to the conclusion that she'd be foolish if she didn't chase up what she'd seen.

Panting and exhausted from his exertions, Ben returned. "Come on, you, enough terrorising the squirrels. Back in the car." The fresh air appeared to have done the trick and enabled her to think straight. There were three people she was desperate to speak to, and they were all within spitting distance of the park. Ruth gave Ben a drink and a treat and then drove to the first house. Eva Lord was just getting ready to leave for her shift at the pub. "Please, Eva, I wouldn't normally ask, it's important I talk to you about this." Ruth showed her the photo she'd captured at the wedding. "Can you explain this?"

The timid brunette gave her a look of resignation as she opened the front door and invited her in. Once they were in the living room, Ruth took a seat on the couch offered to her while Eva remained standing, pacing the floor. "I knew it would only be a matter of time before you came knocking."

"Meaning what? Do you know what happened to Bradley? What's with the hateful expression on your face in the photo?"

Eva's hand covered her heart, and she gasped. "No, you've misunderstood me. I didn't mean that I had killed him, heaven forbid. Would it be wrong of me to think that he got what he deserved?"

"Why don't you tell me what has led you to think that, Eva?"

Eva sighed heavily and threw herself onto the couch beside Ruth. "I'm not the only one to think the way I do about him. I saw it evident in other women there at the wedding."

"I don't doubt that. There are two other women I intend calling on after I see you. What's going on? I can see you're struggling with something. Is the burden lying heavily on your shoulders? Do you think telling me will lead to you getting arrested, is that it?"

Her eyes widened as shock appeared to set in. "I swear I have nothing to feel guilty about. My conscience is perfectly clear. The only thing that doesn't sit well with me is the fact that I'm pleased he's not around any more."

"But why? For the record, that's a pretty callous thing to say. We're talking about a human life."

Eva shook her head, and a small tear dropped onto her cheek. She swiftly swiped it away with the back of her hand. "I don't have to be reminded of that, Ruth. What an insensitive thing to say."

"I'm sorry. All I'm trying to do is search for the truth. This is a murder investigation now, something that I can't take lightly. Okay, I'll stop flinging accusations at you if you promise to tell me what happened between you."

"I can't. I just want the matter to rest now, with him."

"I can't allow that to happen, Eva, you know that. Geraldine deserves answers, you can understand that, can't you? Barely married five minutes before her husband is murdered, how the hell would you react?"

"I know she does. But I don't want to be the one to break the news to her."

"What news? Come on, you're not giving me enough to make an intelligent assumption...wait a minute." She ran a hand over her face and stared at Eva. "You're not telling me he was a sex pest, are you?"

Eva's gaze fell to her clenched hands sitting in her lap. She remained tight-lipped for several seconds, until she finally nodded. "That's exactly what I'm saying. Don't tell me he never tried it on with you?"

"What? No, he didn't." For a fleeting moment, Ruth didn't know if she should be offended or grateful that Bradley hadn't attempted the same with her.

Eva snorted. "You must be the only woman in this town with whom he hasn't tried it on."

Ruth stared at her. "You're kidding me, aren't you?"

Eva vehemently shook her head. "Not in the slightest. Show me the rest of your photos."

Ruth pulled her phone out of her pocket and punched in her password, then she handed it to Eva, who swiped through the photos. Using two fingers to make an image larger, she pointed out the two other women who had caught Ruth's attention prior to her arriving. The women wore a similar expression of distaste whilst looking at Bradley. She continued to swipe through and angled the phone Ruth's way, indicating another couple of women who Ruth had neglected to see.

"There, now tell me I'm alone in thinking he's a sex pest."

Ruth placed her hand over Eva's. "I'm so sorry. I had no idea. Are you up to talking about it? I need to get an idea of what he was up to before I take it any further."

Eva gasped and withdrew her hand. "I'm not willing to take things further. I want the memories to die along with him."

"Is that likely to happen? I can see you're reliving those memories now. It must be torture for you. Won't you consider unburdening yourself?"

Eva inhaled a deep, shuddering breath. "He's badgered me for years."

"Whoa! Years? How many years? Are we talking about before Geraldine and Bradley got together, five years ago?"

"Yep. Once he had you in his sights, there was no stopping him, not until he got what he wanted."

"In what form did this badgering take place? Did he ask you out on a date? More than that?"

"You know I'm a barmaid and what that likely entails from the punters, but somehow his suggestions always seemed lewd and inappropriate. They were always done on the sly, never within earshot of other people."

"Well, this is all news to me. I would never have taken him for a sex pest, not that I disbelieve you, of course. Crap, how am I going to tell Geraldine this?"

Eva quickly clasped her hands. "You can't, I won't allow you. I'll deny everything I've told you here today. I couldn't live with myself if you told her the truth. Why can't you leave things as they are, Ruth?"

"Are you joking? I can't. Geraldine, my best friend in this world, is relying on me to uncover the truth behind her husband's death. Please, don't ask me to keep this from her, I won't do it. She has a right to know what he was like. Surely you can understand that?"

Eva buried her head in her hands and sobbed. When she glanced up at Ruth again, her eyes appeared dead, as if she'd given up. "I won't be able to live with myself if you tell her the truth."

"Don't say that, Eva. I think you'll feel relieved it's all out in the open, take my word on that."

"I can't. I don't want any of this to come out. I've buried it deep within here all these years." She pointed to her head and her heart at the same time.

"Just tell me what happened between you. I swear you'll feel better knowing that it's out in the open."

"I so want to feel better. I haven't had the courage to be with a man since he tried it on with me."

"Please, share the details with me."

Her shoulders slumped. "He pestered me, not like that, but for a date, for months. When I finally relented, we went out. We had a decent time, but when it came to saying goodnight, he wanted to come in for a coffee. We'd both had a bit too much to drink. I thought nothing of it and invited him in. We chatted for a while, everything was fine, as it was during the date. He made me feel special for the first time in my life."

"What changed?" Ruth enquired, urging Eva to go on when she paused.

"He did. It was like a red mist descended. Not at first, granted, but as soon as I slapped his advances away, that's when things got heavy."

"No, you're not telling me he raped you?"

"Thankfully it never came to that. Eventually, he got the message that I wasn't prepared to go further, not on the first date. He stormed off in a huff. After that, he hounded me for months on end to give him another chance. He put his enthusiasm down to the drink he'd consumed that evening. He had a knack of turning the tables, making me feel as though it was all my fault. I felt guilty about that but still refused to cave in to his advances. God, I hate any form of confrontation. He started bad-mouthing me to the punters at work. My boss was livid. Told me to sort him out or I'd get the sack. How the heck do you combat someone with that amount of will and intention?"

"It sounds like you were forced into a corner, put in an untenable position. So, what happened next? Did he eventually get the message?"

"It took months. I was a nervous wreck. I couldn't take the hassle any more and finally told him that if he didn't back off, I would report him to the police. That seemed to do the trick then, although after-wards I was even more nervous. I used to walk home at night after my shift constantly glancing over my shoulder in case he was following me. It was horrendous."

"That's deplorable. I'm so sorry he put you in that position. Maybe if you'd asked your boss to intervene it would have made your life easier."

"I couldn't do that. I'd not been there long. I didn't want to appear weak in my boss's eyes. He would have sacked me. As barmaids, we're supposed to be made of strong stuff. It's expected of us to take a certain amount of good-natured flack from the punters."

"That's dreadful in itself. No wonder you don't see many men working behind the bar down at the Old Swan."

Eva shrugged. "I can't speak for the boss, he has his way of running things. He's all right and treats me fairly on the whole."

"Going back to Bradley, was that the end of the hassle?"

"Yes."

Puzzled, Ruth asked, "If you were that upset with him, what made you attend the wedding?"

"For Geraldine's sake. She's so well-liked around here, it would've been hard if people abandoned the wedding because of that scumbag. Sorry, I shouldn't speak ill of the dead, but that man put me through five or six months of hell that have been, and still are, affecting my whole life. I'm glad he's no longer around to do what he did. I think there will be a lot of relieved women in this town now, or they will be once his funeral is over and done with. I still won't believe he's dead until he's buried six feet under."

"Take my word for it, he's dead, and there is no possible way he could have recovered from that fall."

"Good. I know that makes me sound like a hard, uncaring cow but, under the circumstances, I think it's warranted."

"I couldn't agree with you more. One last thing before I let you get on with your day. If Geraldine is such a good friend, why, oh why, have you never confided in her about what he was like or how he treated you?"

"Would you? If you were in my shoes, could you have thrown a spanner in the works? Maybe he was different with her. I thought he'd changed. It was an eye-opener to me when I glanced around at the other guests and picked out a few women who obviously felt the same way as I did."

"I totally missed it on the day. It wasn't until I looked through the photos today that I picked up on it. Thank you for being so candid with me. I can't thank you enough."

"You're right about one thing. I do feel as though a huge burden has been lifted off my shoulders."

Ruth smiled and patted Eva's hand. "Glad to hear it. Why don't you be kind to yourself and go the whole hog and take time out to work through your feelings with a counsellor? I also feel I need to add that not all men are the same."

"You appear to be very happy with James. Any plans on tying the knot yourself in the future?"

"That's like asking how long a piece of string is. I love him far more than I've ever loved another man. I'm simply struggling to commit. He asks me constantly, and each time I reject him I see another crack develop in our relationship. I don't want to be forced into a marriage that might go wrong further down the line."

"I can understand that. I think your doubts are realistic. I'm sure hundreds of women who are in a relationship feel the same way. Sadly, I'm not likely to be in that position myself."

"Nonsense. Think positively going forward and get some help. You've done it once, spoken to me about the bad experience you encountered, so listening to the advice of a counsellor will put you on the right track, I'm sure. If not, you have my permission to punch me in the face."

They both laughed as they rose from their seats. Eva led her to the door and surprised Ruth by giving her a suffocating hug.

"Thank you, Ruth. I hope you find the perpetrator. I'm dying to hear the outcome of your investigation and what this person's motive was for doing away with him."

"Top of my list when I discover who the culprit is. I won't give up until I nail the person. If you hear any snippets of gossip down at the pub, you know where I am. Take care, Eva."

"I will, Ruth, you can be sure of that. Thank you for listening to my woes, it really made a difference."

"You're welcome. Stop being so hard on yourself and get on with your life. If you take my advice, you should join a club or something. Don't go dating any of the punters from the pub."

"Excellent advice. I was wondering whether to enrol in the new tango class at the town hall. Do you know if it's popular?"

"No idea, sorry. Or, you could join the Am-Dram club. We hold regular meetings every Sunday evening."

"That's a thought. My acting skills aren't up to much, I'm afraid."

"Not a problem. You could always join to be part of what goes on behind the scenes. Think about it and give me a call. We'd love you to join us. We do tend to gossip like old women at times, but we have a laugh. That's the main thing in this life, isn't it?"

"I must admit, I've not done a lot of that over the years. Thanks for the suggestion, I'll seriously consider it and get back to you. I'm a little shy with new things as an outsider."

"No need. All the members probably frequent the pub anyway, so they won't be strangers to you."

"Now you've got my juices going. It would be better than tango classes—I'd need a male partner for that, which is out of the question…for now," Eva added before Ruth could open her mouth.

"Good. Let me know."

CHAPTER 10

Her stomach churning with a mixture of outrage and disgust, Ruth drove to the next woman's house. Unfortunately, Maria Fox wasn't at home. However, Ruth wasn't going to let that alter her plans about speaking to her. She hopped back in the car and pulled up outside the small supermarket in town where Maria worked. That was the beauty of living in a small community—most of the time, people knew where everyone else worked.

Upon entering the Cove Supermarket, she saw the manager, Lee Oswald, stacking the shelves with cans of beans. "Hi, Lee. Nice to see you getting your hands dirty for a change." She smiled down at him.

"Oi, you. I'll have you know that I'm always on the shop floor tinkering with this or that."

Ruth raised an inquisitive eyebrow. "Not the best response you could have made. Lucky there's no one else around to overhear your remark."

He shook his head and stood. "What do you want, Ruth?"

"Sorry, I'm only teasing, you know me."

"Yep, that I do. A pain in the rear at the best of times." He smirked.

"Whatever. I'll let that one slip, for now. I was wondering, in my official capacity as the town's only PI, if I could have a chat with Maria for ten minutes or so."

He peered over his shoulder at the pretty blonde cashier. "Is she in some kind of trouble? Should I be concerned? Do I have a murderer working for me?"

Ruth cringed when she heard the final question. For all she knew, he could be right. Many a true word spoken in jest and all that. "None of the above. I will say one thing, Lee. You have an overactive imagination."

He chuckled. "If you're ever hiring, I'm your man."

His chuckle proved infectious, and in spite of trying to keep a straight face, she burst out laughing at the camp tone he'd used. "I'll bear that in mind."

"I'll relieve her on the till. We're the only two on duty. You can go through to the staffroom and have a chat there. She's not likely to be upset, is she?"

Ruth hitched up a shoulder. "I really don't know is the honest answer. I'll be as gentle as I can with my questions."

He peered over his shoulder a second time and leaned in. "Can I have a hint?"

She mimicked him and whispered, "About anything in particular?" She laughed.

"You always were a tease, even during our schooldays. It's not too late for me to rescind my acceptance, you know."

Lee had always been a dear friend from the minute they attended their first day at school together. There wasn't a week that went by when she didn't tease him in some way. She regularly did her top-up shopping here during the week. "You look on the verge of tears," she teased him further.

"Get outta here. You've got ten minutes. Use it wisely, ratbag."

"Charming. Do your bosses know you call your customers names?"

He let out an exasperated sigh. "You never fail to deliver a sharp retort. I'm surprised your mouth isn't cut to shreds with that sharp tongue of yours."

She squeezed his chubby cheeks. "You say the nicest things. Can you take over from her now? Time is money in my job."

They walked back towards the checkout together. "Cut the your-job-is-better-than-mine routine."

"I wasn't aware that I intimated anything of the sort." She grinned like a crazed chimp.

"Maria, I'll take over from you. Miss Marple here would like to grill you in the staffroom over something she's not prepared to divulge."

Ruth's elbow connected with his ribs, making him grunt. "Ignore him, I'd just like an informal chat about something—if you're willing to see me, that is?"

"About what?"

Ruth's glance flew between Lee and Maria. She sighed. "It's a personal matter."

It didn't go unnoticed that the colour instantly drained from her face. "Really? About what? Oh, I think I can guess."

Ruth stepped to the side and motioned for Maria to lead the way, away from Lee's flapping ears. "We shouldn't be too long. Then you can get back to stacking your shelves. And there was me thinking a store manager's role was an important one."

He snorted. "You'd be the first to bloomin' complain if the shelves were empty when you popped in."

Ruth grinned. "You're not wrong there. We won't be long, I promise."

Maria raced ahead of her. Ruth had to trot to keep up with the woman who was in her late twenties and wearing higher than normal footwear for a shop worker. She got a whiff of the young woman's fragrant perfume but couldn't put a name to the orange-scented odour.

She followed Maria through the open doorway, past the stock-room and into a pokey kitchen area that had a small table and two chairs over to one side.

Maria plonked down in one of the chairs. "Will this take long?"

"No. I already told you that. Although it depends on what you can tell me."

"Not a lot. I was there as a guest, along with the hundred or so other people from the town," she replied defensively.

"Okay. First of all, can I say that you can cut the attitude? No one is accusing you of anything. This is only a general enquiry. Yes, Geraldine has employed me to find out what happened to Bradley, but it's this I really want to talk to you about." She flipped out her phone and showed Maria the photo she'd taken of her at the reception.

Maria gasped, and the colour that had dissipated in her cheeks a few minutes earlier came flooding back. "It's a photo. What about it?"

"It was a wedding, and you were caught glaring at the groom."

She held her palms up in front of her. "I can't see the groom anywhere in the picture, can you?"

"Come on, Maria, I'm not daft. If it's any consolation, I've been speaking to Eva Lord. Whilst I can't tell you what she said, I can show you this." She swiped through her phone and found the photo she'd taken of Eva, and then, to enforce what she was saying, went on to show her the photos of the other women she'd caught on camera, all wearing a similar expression.

"So what? Not everyone can pin a smile in place twenty-four-seven."

"Granted. Maria, I'm not here to judge you. All I want to know is why? If you clearly despised Bradley so much, why did you go to the wedding?"

"It wasn't him who invited me, it was Geraldine. She's my friend, has been for years, why shouldn't I have gone to the wedding?"

"Can you tell me why you hated Bradley? Bearing in mind that I've just this minute had a similar conversation with Eva."

Her gaze dropped to the table, and she fell silent.

Ruth reached across to touch her hand. "You're not alone, I promise you. I can help ease the pain you're feeling. The pain you've felt for years by the look of things. Please, Maria, confide in me. A problem shared and all that."

She shook her head, and a small cluster of tears dripped onto her cheeks. Ruth's heart went out to the young woman. In that instant, she detested Bradley even more than she had when he'd been alive. She knew what these women were hiding to protect Geraldine's feelings. All right, Bradley had never abused her in the past, but she had been on the end of his vile tongue lashings at times.

Maria sniffled and stood to collect a piece of kitchen towel off the countertop. She returned to her seat, dabbed at her eyes and blew her nose. "He was a horrible man. The only way I can describe him really was similar to a chameleon. I can't believe that Geraldine wasn't able to see through him. To me he was super-transparent at the best and worst of times."

Ruth nodded. "What did he do to you, love?"

"Nothing. Not physically as such. Maybe the odd touch across the backside at a nightclub now and again. I challenged him a few times, but he was always adamant that he hadn't done anything." She shuddered. "The creepy thing is, and I could never prove it, I always felt it wasn't his hands doing the touching, if you get my drift?"

Ruth's mouth hung open for a moment or two until she said, "Another part of his anatomy? Like the thing that resides in his trousers?"

Maria shuddered again in response. "What a despicable pipsqueak he was. Did Eva say the same?"

"Something similar along those lines. I can't go into specific details, though. Poor you. When did it start?"

"I can't give you actual dates. What I can tell you is that he was engaged to Geraldine when he started coming on to me."

"Coming on to you? Did he ever suggest you go out together?"

"Go out? No. He was more to the point than that. He told me on more than one occasion that he thought we could make wonderful music together. What a creep."

Ruth shook her head in disgust and sighed heavily. "Why didn't you tell Geraldine?"

Her gaze lifted to meet Ruth's. "I did. Oh, it was years ago on a drunken night out together. She pooh-poohed it, so I never mentioned it again. He was all over the girls when he was let out on his own at night. He must have stunk of perfume when he got home. If she chose to ignore the clues, time and time again, she was unlikely to listen to her friends slating him, was she?"

"A case of love being blind, is that what you're suggesting?"

"Yes, that's exactly what I meant. I wish I'd had the courage to raise the topic again. I didn't, and that's the end of it. She was smitten, head over heels in love with him. In her eyes, he couldn't do a thing wrong."

"That's so sad. I understand where you're coming from. Bradley and I have had a fraught relationship over the years, shall we say? Except everything was hunky dory in front of Geraldine. It's hard trying to shield your friend. I know you spoke out, but you admitted it was on a drunken night out. Maybe you should have returned to the topic in the cold light of day."

"Hey, you can pack that in. Don't lay the blame at my door for this. You're not suggesting that I killed him, are you?" she asked, her voice rising through the octaves.

"No. Not at all. But someone did."

"Do you seriously think it could be a woman? One of those you photographed?" she cried in disbelief.

"I honestly don't know at this point. Did you see anything at the wedding? Bradley trying it on with someone else perhaps? Anything along those lines?"

Maria fell silent for a moment and then shook her head. "I can't say I saw anything suspicious. Up until the murder happened, everyone was having a good time, despite what you caught on your camera."

"Okay, are you telling me that Bradley was still abusing you right up to his death?"

"I wouldn't necessarily say he was abusing me. He tried it on. I was upset, and my brother caught me crying one day, asked me what the problem was. I broke down and told him; I was so depressed by that point. He took it upon himself to have a word with Bradley. He didn't have to do much. He backed off immediately once Sean had a word in his ear. Men are such cowards when confronted by other men, aren't they?"

Ruth smiled. "I'm glad Sean intervened before anything too drastic happened to you. Did you speak to Bradley at the wedding? I can't say I noticed the two of you in conversation on the day."

"No. I kept my distance. Good job he wasn't clingy with Geraldine on Saturday. I managed to offer my congratulations to her while he was chatting to a bunch of his mates. He really did give me the creeps after he tried it on. I can't say I felt that way about him before that. Strange how an incident like that can do so much damage to a relationship, not that we really had one in the first place. Oh gosh, I'm talking in riddles now. You see what the damn man does to me?"

"Don't worry about it. I get what you mean. Do you think it's possible one of the other women had difficulties with him and perhaps told her partner and he took things into his own hands?"

"Who knows? All I know is that my brother was incensed. He's a gentleman, though, when it comes to treating a woman right."

"Glad to hear it. James is the same," she added, a familiar pang of guilt touching her heart.

"Not many around nowadays. I've just started dating Colin Cosgrove. He seems decent enough; early days yet."

"Try not to let the negativity of your past affect your future happiness with your new fella."

"I'm trying hard. It's very difficult at times. Is that all? I bet Lee's wondering where I am." She wiped her eyes on another sheet of kitchen towel. "Do I still look like a panda?"

"Nope, you're as beautiful as the day you were born. Not that I know that, of course, figuratively speaking."

"You are funny. I feel bad not being able to help you. I hope you're able to give Geraldine the answers she's searching for. I know it's a terrible thing to say, but in my heart I'm glad she won't be tied to him for the rest of her life. She was far too good for him. He had some kind of spell over her that none of us were privy to, that's all I can say."

Ruth left her seat and followed Maria out of the staffroom and back into the shop. "I think you're right there, Maria. Thank you again for being so honest with me. I'm sorry you experienced the worst that man could offer."

"We all have our crosses to bear in this life. I think I'll be a lot happier knowing he's not around to hinder what lies ahead of me."

"Thank you, Mrs Knowles. See you next week." Lee had finished serving one of the local pensioners and was holding the door open for her when they arrived. He'd obviously had an ear trained on their conversation, because as soon as the door shut behind Mrs Knowles, he asked, "Who's not around any more?"

Ruth shook her head and winked at Maria who had slipped into her position behind the counter. "Nice try, Lee. Thanks for standing in while Maria and I had a very informative chat," she teased, whisking past him and leaving the shop.

She suppressed the giggle dying to escape and rushed back to her car. Ben welcomed her with a lick to the ear. She stopped off again at the park so he could stretch his legs. "I've never known a dog get as many trips to the park as you, boy. I hope you're grateful."

Ben barked as if understanding what she'd said and bounded after a squirrel he spotted out of the corner of his eye. Ruth laughed; however, as she reflected on the conversations she'd had with the two women that afternoon, her blood boiled. She couldn't help wondering why Geraldine had chosen to ignore what Maria had tried to tell her about Bradley. Was it really because she was head over heels in love with the man? Or something else? Geraldine had always been a little insecure in her eyes. Boyfriends had come and gone in the past, a few dates with one guy before she'd moved on to the next. *Bradley had been her only lasting relationship, why? Was she in fear of being left on the shelf? Don't be so ridiculous. Of course it wasn't because of that, or was it?*

After Ben had run around for fifteen minutes, excitedly greeting several other dogs he often met, Ruth slipped his leash on and jumped back in the car.

Instead of returning to the office, knowing that the business line had been diverted to her mobile and no calls had come through, she decided to head home for the day.

Feeling guilty for the way she'd treated James over the last day or so, she decided he and the boys deserved a treat and removed four steaks from the freezer along with a bag of chips. Then she peeled some mushrooms and onions and cut a few tomatoes in half.

Thirty minutes later, Carolyn walked through the back door. Ruth gathered her sister in her arms and guided her to a chair at the table, forcing her to sit. "You look dead on your feet. How's Keith?"

"I am. I slept in the chair beside his bed all night in case he woke up. I needn't have bothered, he slept right through, unlike me. Crikey, hospitals can be so noisy during the night. I guess I'd forgotten all about that from my spells in hospital when having the kids."

"Bless you. I'll put the water on. You can have a nice soak in the bath. Damn, we're having steak tonight, and I've only got four. That's no problem, though, I'll cut an inch or so off each one when they're cooked. We'll get by."

Carolyn laughed. "You're so practical. I would've freaked out if I were in your shoes. Oh, and Keith is grumpy as hell, by the way. That's why I came home early. Couldn't stand him moaning about what else he should be doing at the house rather than spending enforced time in a hospital bed. Men! They're hopeless, aren't they?"

"Most of the time, yes. Look on the bright side—it doesn't sound like he'll be in hospital that long."

Carolyn rolled her eyes. "I think that's when our real problems will start, when he comes home, except we haven't really got a home for him to come home to." Her head dropped into her hands, and she sobbed.

Her sons chose that moment to walk through the back door. "Mum, Mum, what is it? Dad's okay, isn't he? He's not..."

Carolyn uncovered her face and smiled at her sons. "He's fine. Mummy is exhausted and feeling a tad overwhelmed by everything, boys, don't worry. How was school?"

"The pits," Ian said, pressing himself against his mum. "Can we visit Dad tonight?"

"Maybe tomorrow. Your mum has only just come home from the hospital. Go and wash up, boys, dinner won't be long," Ruth intervened, knowing what Carolyn was like and how easily she gave in to her sons when they wanted something.

Ian and Robin picked up the bags they'd dropped when the concern had consumed them for their mother and left the room.

"I feel so sorry for them. The disruption these damn renovations must be having on their schoolwork. We're selfish, aren't we? We have to be to put them through all this turmoil and angst. It's not their fault they're without a proper roof over their heads, it's *ours*."

"Hey, they've never complained to me. You're being too hard on yourself, as usual. Come on, help me prepare the rest of the dinner, it'll take your mind off things."

Carolyn left the table and went straight to the drawer to collect the cutlery. "I'll lay the table. Looks like you have everything else in hand. Oh, Ian doesn't like tomatoes by the way."

"Thanks for telling me that, more for us."

As soon as James came home, Ruth began cooking the meal. The smell of rump steak drifted through the house, acting like a bullhorn for the boys, calling them downstairs and into the kitchen.

Sitting at the table with a feast in front of them, Carolyn nudged both boys. "You don't get treated this well at home, boys, do you?"

The boys shook their heads and then ripped into their steak.

"You'll soon be home and back to normal in a few months," Ruth said, feeling slightly smug that she'd successfully managed to supply enough dinner for all of them in spite of her sister's unexpected arrival.

Carolyn insisted on clearing away the plates and washing up while Ruth divided the lemon cheesecake and served it with ice cream. The boys went crazy over their dessert. They both finished it in record time and asked to be excused so they could go back upstairs to complete their homework.

The adults took their coffee through to the lounge.

Carolyn sighed when she sank into the couch. "This feels good on my bones."

"Don't get too comfortable, you should go and have a soak in the bath soon."

"Thanks, I definitely need that. I'll just finish my coffee first. Hey, how's the case going?"

Ruth shrugged. "It's going. Let's say that more and more pieces of the puzzle slotted into place today."

"Care to enlighten us as to what that cryptic comment is about?" James asked, leaning forward to peer around Carolyn.

"I can't say at the moment. If all of this comes out, I think we're going to have dozens of people with a motive we can put on our list of suspects."

"Sounds intriguing and scary at the same time. Right, I'm going up for a bath. Thanks for taking care of us so well, Ruth. I promise we won't outstay our welcome." Carolyn bent over and kissed Ruth on the cheek then left the room.

Once the door was closed behind her, James swapped seats to sit next to Ruth. "Come on, spill. What have you managed to find out?"

"I'll tell you on one proviso."

"What's that?"

"That it goes no further. If Littlejohn persists in not chasing up what the guests have to say, then that's her lookout. She's missing a trick."

"Deal, and I agree. For some reason she appears to be neglecting her duties on this case."

Ruth gasped as a thought went through her mind. "No, you don't think it's because Geraldine is my best friend?"

"Who knows? Tell me what you've found out."

Ruth spent the next ten minutes filling James in about the interviews she'd had during the day. "So, that's it in a nutshell. I think there are far more women in this community who could probably tell similar tales. I just need to find them. Are you telling me that you've never heard anything of this nature attributed to Bradley?"

"No, nothing. Sounds as though he was a sick individual. In my experience, men like that tend to distance themselves from other men. Are you saying that it's possible one of these women could have pushed him?"

"Honestly, no, I don't think either Eva or Maria could have done it.

But that doesn't mean to say another woman he might have touched up didn't kill him. I have to admit, if he'd tried it on with me, I would have killed him long ago."

James' mouth hung open for a second or two before he replied, "You don't mean that?"

"I do. You should have seen the way Eva, in particular, broke down today. She's lived with him stalking her for years."

"Stalking her? I'd hardly call it that."

"Wouldn't you? I would. He was a flaming sex pest who was allowed to get away with ruining several women's lives. Shame on him. It's Geraldine who I feel sorry for. I don't think she had a clue what he was really like. How the dickens am I going to tell her?"

"I'm sorry. I don't have any answers for you to that particular dilemma."

"I can't help wondering how many Evas and Marias are out there. How many women did he either abuse or hassle over the years? Don't forget the other reports I'm looking into regarding the football team. By all accounts, he was a despicable man who someone should have had the courage to bring to task when he was alive."

"Instead, they took their revenge by ending his life!"

"So it would appear."

CHAPTER 11

CAROLYN TOOK over the school run the following day, leaving Ruth to get back to her usual routine. Before she set off for the office, she took Ben for a walk along her favoured spot, the coastal path. The sea was a little rough this morning, thrashing and foaming against the rocky shoreline below as the wind got up. The weatherman on breakfast TV had warned that rain would come in this afternoon, hence Ruth taking the opportunity to give Ben a run first thing. She always felt guilty when he didn't get at least one run a day.

She smiled, watching her treasured companion running ahead and then trotting back to see where she was. During the walk, she mentally noted down a few things on her virtual to-do list. She hadn't managed to get much sleep all night and had decided to go back to Carmel Cove Hall to speak with Lady Falkirk. She hoped that the lady of the manor would grant her permission to speak with the staff who had been on duty on Saturday. Perhaps they'd seen or overheard something. But then, if they had, why hadn't they come forward by now?

Ben was panting heavily when she fastened him into his harness. She filled up his water bowl and held it while he lapped at the cold liquid, splashing it over her hand and the seat. "Thanks for sharing it around, buddy, most considerate of you."

She drove up to Carmel Cove Hall and found the butler, Mr Wells, standing at the entrance. He turned her way and glanced at her in his usual offhand manner, treating her as if she was something he'd stepped in.

She opened the windows a little for Ben and locked the car. "Hello, Mr Wells. Sorry to drop by unannounced. Any chance I can have a brief chat with Lady Falkirk?"

"I wouldn't have thought so. She never deals with unexpected guests."

"I apologise again. It's really important I see her."

"I'll do that later, not now. Make sure the bedrooms are aired for the guests arriving this afternoon," Lady Falkirk ordered one of the staff as she appeared in the doorway. "Hello, Ruth. How lovely to see you. Do you have time for a quick cup of coffee?"

"Hello, Lady Falkirk, that would be divine, thank you." She smiled at Lady Falkirk and then at Mr Wells, who appeared to be seething under his usual frosty exterior.

"Wells, arrange for some coffee and biscuits to be brought to the parlour immediately, there's a good man."

"Yes, m'lady." Wells marched into the house, the tails of his coat swishing from side to side like an angry lion's tail.

"Come in, dear. Looks like rain. Still, we mustn't grumble, the weather has been good for months, for a change."

"It has. Thank you for seeing me, Lady Falkirk."

Ruth followed Lady Falkirk through the house to the sophisticatedly dressed parlour. Sage-coloured velvet curtains framed each of the grand windows at both ends of the room. There was a large open stone fireplace which was the focal point of the expansive parlour. The décor was simply stunning. Subtle pinks and reds covered the walls, making it a cosy environment to enjoy.

Once they were seated in the rose-coloured Queen Anne chairs, Lady Falkirk asked, "What brings you here today, Ruth? Oh my, where are my manners? How is your dear friend?"

"Geraldine is bearing up." She cringed. How did she even know that? What with what had happened with Keith and interviewing the wedding guests, it had been days since she'd contacted Geraldine. She made a mental note to do that as soon as she left Carmel Cove Hall.

"I'm glad to hear that. What a terrible incident it was, all the more so when it took place on the poor girl's wedding day."

"She'll survive. She's made of strong stuff, is Geraldine."

"That's good to know. So, why are you visiting me today?"

"I was wondering if you'd allow me to have a brief chat with your staff."

"Gosh, of course. I should've allowed you to have carried out some interviews before now, how silly of me. I'm so caught up with organising my day around here, the tiniest detail seems to slip my mind."

"No need to apologise. I did stop by a few days ago, but everyone was rushing around so I decided to call back another time. I really can't leave it much longer, not when there's a murderer on the loose. Most people have a tendency to think about the victim and forget about trying to capture the assailant."

"Count me as one of them. Of course, let's have our coffee first. Ah, here it is now."

A maid wearing a black uniform and white lace, tiara-like hat entered the room and deposited the tray on the small coffee table.

"Thank you, Sarah. I'll see to it now."

Sarah left the room, and Lady Falkirk poured the coffee. She handed a china cup and saucer to Ruth and then a plateful of shortbread biscuits.

Ruth struggled to resist the temptation to sample one of her favourite biscuits. "Thank you, they look delicious."

"They are. My friend ships them down from Edinburgh for me. That reminds me, I only have a couple of packets left, and my guests simply adore them. I shall need to put in another request for the delectable snacks. Tell me about the case, Ruth? I'm intrigued to know how your job works. Do you work alongside the police?"

Ruth chuckled. "Hardly, Lady Falkirk. I believe sometimes the local inspector regards me as more of a hindrance than a help. Probably because nine times out of ten I solve the crimes sooner than she does."

"Really? How fascinating. Why is that, dear?"

"Because I'm tenacious, I suppose. Once I have the bit between my teeth, there's very little that will deter me from getting to the truth."

Lady Falkirk punched her fist in the air, rattling her cup and saucer at the same time. "Good for you. Power to the little people. Do you find your tenacity gets you into bother with the police?"

Ruth twisted her mouth. "Occasionally. It doesn't bother me, though. The necessity to uncover the truth is what drives me forward."

"Excellent. Well, drink up, dear, and I'll introduce you to the staff —a proper introduction—and then you can go from there. I must admit, none of them have mentioned to me they saw anything untoward on Saturday, but then I didn't ask. I suppose I was in a state of shock for a few days after the incident occurred. To think, this place now has the reputation of being a murder scene." Her hand touched her cheek. "No, I won't allow myself to think of such dreadful details. I can do without the added drama in my life, that's for certain."

"I'm sorry it happened here. I hope it doesn't taint the way people think of your beautiful home, Lady Falkirk."

"I hope so too, dear."

Ruth drained her cup and placed it back on the silver tray.

"Okay, let's see if we can sort you out a room to use." Lady Falkirk raised her finger. "I know the exact room. Come with me."

Ruth followed Lady Falkirk through the large hallway and down a narrow corridor. She flung open the door to an expansive library. "Will this do you?"

The room took Ruth's breath away. Floor-to-ceiling bookcases lined the room with a ladder on each side attached to the bookcases themselves. She could imagine a child playing in here endlessly, for hours. "It's breathtaking."

"Thank you. I designed it myself and had it commissioned a few years ago. Pretty damned expensive, not that I'm one for talking about money much, you understand."

"I can imagine. I bet this room cost more to design and fill than my cottage is worth."

Lady Falkirk laughed. "I fear you may be right about that, dear. Now, who would you like to interview first?"

"It really doesn't matter. Whoever is available. Thank you, Lady Falkirk."

"No need for thanks. If it'll help to reveal the culprit, then I'm only too willing to oblige." She left the room.

Ruth couldn't resist it. She walked over to the bookcase and ran her fingers lovingly along the dust-free shelves. *They must be a nightmare to keep clean.* She nipped back to the antique desk in the corner of the room and pulled her notebook and pen out of her pocket then sat down.

There was a slight knock on the door, and it opened to reveal a plump lady in her sixties. "I've been told to come and see you. I'm the housekeeper."

"Come in. It's Mrs Chambers, isn't it? I think your husband services my car at the local garage."

"That's me. What can I do for you today? I requested to be the first because I have several rooms to make up for her ladyship who has yet more guests arriving. They're coming out of the woodwork at the moment, all because of this murder, I'm betting."

"More than likely. I won't keep you long. Were you at the wedding on Saturday?"

"Sadly not. Therefore, I can't help you."

"Maybe not regarding the day itself, but maybe you've heard some gossip in town that you think might help me."

Mrs Chambers laughed. "You must be desperate if you're starting to rely on gossip, dear."

"Not really. Going by past experience, I know how important it is to listen to what's being said locally."

"I'm sorry, I've heard nothing. Not a scrap to be honest with you. Will that be all? I've got tons to do now that the SOCO team have finished upstairs. I couldn't touch the place for a few days."

"If I give you one of my cards, will you ring me if you do hear anything?"

"Of course. Good luck. Must fly."

She watched the woman scurry out of the room. The door closed and was immediately reopened by a timid-looking young woman in her early twenties, who hesitated in the doorway.

"Come in. I promise not to bite."

She walked across the room, sat in the chair next to Ruth and placed her hands in her lap. "I'm Samantha Shaw."

"Good to meet you, Samantha. Are you from around here?"

"No, I live a few miles away in Lunder. I travel to work every day."

"I didn't think I recognised you. I'm the local private investigator. The bride has employed me to try and find out who killed her husband. Were you working on Saturday?"

"Yes. I was based mostly in the marquee."

"Did you happen to overhear anything that you have since thought of as suspicious on the day?"

The young woman stared at Ruth and shook her head. "No. I really can't say I have. We were all so busy on the day, flying around here, there and everywhere, attending to the guests, ensuring they had a good time."

"I understand. Maybe you've heard something since that day you'd like to share with me?"

"No. Nothing. I would if I knew anything, I promise."

Ruth could tell the young woman was telling the truth. "Thank you for seeing me. Can you send the next person in on your way out?"

"Sorry I couldn't help you," Samantha apologised then left the room.

Ruth stared down at her empty notebook. *I hope this doesn't turn out to be a waste of time.*

Footsteps on the nearby floorboards broke into her thoughts. Ruth smiled at the young brunette walking towards her.

"Hello, and you are?"

"Belinda Swallow, ma'am."

"Ruth will do just fine. Please take a seat, I won't keep you long. Were you on duty at the wedding on Saturday?"

Her head dropped. "Yes."

"Where were you stationed?"

"Mostly around the main hall, topping up the guests' drinks."

Belinda was very shy and quietly spoken, almost to the point of Ruth struggling to hear some of her answers properly. "Did you see what happened?"

"No. I was on a quick break at the time. I reappeared when I heard the screams."

"As you were on duty in the main hall, can you recall seeing anyone go up the main staircase at all?"

"Only the man who died, Miss."

"Are you sure no one else went up there?"

She shrugged. "They might have done, but I didn't see them."

"That's a shame. Maybe you overheard an argument or something along those lines on the day?"

"No. Nothing. I was too busy to listen to other people's arguments or conversations."

"I suppose so."

With that, the door opened, and the butler stuck his head into the room. "All finished in here? I have a job for Belinda that needs her urgent attention."

Ruth narrowed her eyes at Mr Wells. "Okay, I think I'm done. There's nothing else you can tell me, Belinda?"

Belinda's gaze drifted over to the door and back to Ruth. She hurriedly stood and mumbled an apology before she rushed out of the room. Mr Wells disappeared with her.

Again, Ruth looked down at the blank page. She quickly drew a rabbit that one of the kids at school had taught her years ago, just so the blank page stopped tormenting her.

Another young woman entered the room. She was blonde, her long hair tied back in a ponytail. "Is this going to take long?" she demanded, chewing on a piece of gum. "I'm guessing not after the others left quickly."

"Unfortunately, I think I must have called on the wrong day. Everyone seems so busy at the moment."

"Yeah, we are. I'm willing to hang around for a bit, if that's what you want. My feet could do with a rest."

Ruth smiled. "Let's hope Mr Wells doesn't call you away too soon then. It's Sarah, isn't it?" she asked, remembering what Lady Falkirk had called her when she'd brought them a drink.

"Sarah Wallender. I doubt it. I'm hardly his favourite around here. Anyway, what Daddy wants, Daddy gets, right?"

Frowning, Ruth asked, "Sorry, I don't understand. Is that comment supposed to mean something?"

"Belinda is his daughter."

"Oh right. I didn't make the connection because of the different surnames. Is Belinda married?"

"Yes, she got married last year."

"Ah okay. So he tends to favour her when he has a specific job in mind because she's his daughter, is that what you're saying?"

"Well done. Full marks for your observations and following the clues."

Ruth felt the colour rise in her cheeks. "Okay, back to business. Were you on duty the day of the wedding?"

"I was. Flitting here and there like a good 'un. Worn out by mid-afternoon, I was, but we weren't allowed to have a break, although some of the more privileged among us seemed to achieve that."

"You're referring to Belinda again? If you have any grievances, why don't you take them to Lady Falkirk?"

"Would you? Wells would come down heavy on me if I did that. Best not to say anything and keep my head down. Jobs are getting scarce around these parts. Have you seen the unemployment statistics for small towns and villages?"

"Not lately, no. Can I ask if you either saw anything or overheard something on the day that you shouldn't have?"

"That's a bit obscure. Oh right, you're talking about the murder. Forgive me, my brain is still in bed until lunchtime some days."

"Not a problem. I should have made my question clearer. Anything?"

"Not really. Can't think of anything of use. Have you got any suspects? Maybe it was an old flame that threw him off that turret."

"Did you know Bradley?"

"Not as such. Seen him around a few of the nightclubs in other towns. Likes to get close to women, shall we say?"

Her interest levels went off the radar. "He does? In what respect?"

"You'll have to use your imagination."

Ruth inclined her head. "Are you telling me that he liked to grope women?"

Sarah lifted one of her shoulders but said nothing.

"Sarah, are you telling me that he touched you up?"

"He might have, once or twice over the years, but he got a slap around the face for his trouble."

Ruth smirked. "Good for you. I think I'd react in the same way."

"I feel sorry for the poor cow who married him. Fancy having a letch like that as your husband."

"When was the last time you had problems with him?"

"Gawd, now you're asking. Around three months ago. My boyfriend saw him groping a girl at a nightclub and pinned him up against the wall."

"Wow! That was brave of him."

"Not really. He was livid when I told him that Bradley had done the same to me. Threatened to go round there to punch his lights out the second the words left my lips. I persuaded him not to. That didn't stop him ploughing in there when he saw the weasel grope a young girl at the nightclub while she was dancing."

"What happened afterwards?" Ruth jotted down the information.

"The bouncers intervened and told them both to either break it up or they'd be thrown out and banned. I pulled Tyson away, and that was the end of it."

"Tyson, as in Mike Tyson?"

"Yep, his dad insisted he be named after the boxer. Might be why he loves going down the gym to work out."

"Does Tyson have a surname?"

"Of course. It's Brown. Tyson Brown."

"Where does he work?"

"At the gym in Lunder. Spends most of his time on the equipment rather than dealing with the punters. Loves having a 'physique most people would envy'. His words, not mine, although I'm not complaining." Sarah sniggered, imitating a teenage girl talking about her first crush.

"You've been really helpful so far, Sarah. Can you think of anything else I should know?"

She shook her head. "I don't think so."

Ruth stood and offered her hand.

Sarah shook it firmly and left the room, shouting over her shoulder, "I hope you get the person responsible for this. It's not nice living in an area where there's a killer on the loose."

"Don't I know it?" Ruth said under her breath. She gathered her notebook and pen together and said goodbye to her salubrious surroundings with a tinge of regret.

Mr Wells was in the hall, ordering the staff what to do next. She waited until he'd finished talking and sent the staff on their way. "Thank you for allowing me to speak to them, Mr Wells. I don't suppose you can spare me five minutes?"

"No. I'm very sorry. I'm going to be at full speed for the rest of the day. I'll see you out, Miss." He turned on his heel. His shoes were shined to perfection. The man obviously took pride in his job and his appearance. He waited at the front door for her to catch up.

Ruth handed him a card. "When you get five minutes, I'd love to have a chat."

He took the card and placed it in his shirt pocket. "If I get the time. Good day, Miss."

She smiled and hopped back in the car. When she reversed, Mr Wells was still standing at the entrance.

What's he think I'm going to do, turn back and rob the silver?

She waved. His response was to nod before he closed the large front door.

Ruth blew out a frustrated breath and began her journey to the office. "Well, that was a waste of time, Ben. I've had more fulfilling days recently, I can tell you." He moaned and looked at her in the rear-view mirror. "All right, you win, maybe a brief detour is in order. Only a five-minute run around the park. I have work to do, like ringing Tyson, although I'm tempted to go and see him. He's got a fantastic physique apparently, not that I'm interested in that type of thing. I've got James. He's fit enough for me, more than I can handle at times. Oops…too much information for your young, sensitive ears."

They reached the park. Cynthia was there with her poodle, which meant their quick visit was extended to accommodate Ben's flirting with his new lady friend. What a cute couple they'd be if they ever got together.

Nonsense, I've got enough trouble on my plate right now, without running around trying to get a couple of dogs to mate!

CHAPTER 12

WHEN SHE RANG TYSON, he recapped what Sarah had said virtually word for word but regrettably couldn't add anything further of interest. Ruth went back to the wedding guest list and rang several more people. Unfortunately, her earlier frustrations came flooding back and multiplied in the process.

Ruth was treating herself to a ten-minute break and enjoying a cup of rich, strong coffee when her phone rang. "Hello, Carmel Cove Detective Agency, how may I help you?"

"Ruth, it's me."

"Hi, Louise, tell me you managed to find something out? I've been struggling all day and I'm in the process of losing the will to live."

"Nope, sorry. I found nothing in the archives."

"Bummer, I was hoping you would."

"Unfortunately not, but don't lose heart just yet. I do have some news for you that I think you'll find interesting."

Ruth sat upright in her chair. "Go on, I'm all ears."

"I asked around the office to see if any of the other reporters knew Bradley Sinclair or if his name rang a bell, and Greg, he's been here for over five years now, came up with the goods."

"Go on. I'm dying to hear the gossip."

"Well, he remembers Bradley being in some kind of trouble with some of the parents of the lads on the local football team. One day, a few of the fathers cornered Bradley—warned him not to be so demanding of their sons. Apparently, he ruled the training a tad harshly shall we say, although Greg likened Bradley's form of discipline to an ancient time when, if someone did something wrong, they faced a den of lions."

"Are you kidding me? These were young boys. No one had a right to treat them like that."

"You're not wrong there. That's why several of the fathers took things into their own hands."

"That's interesting. One question: why on earth didn't the fathers report him to someone on the council if they were playing for the county team?"

She laughed. "You know what men are like. Most of them prefer to go down the heavy-handed route to get their point across. Maybe they thought they'd sort things out themselves, without involving the authorities."

"Wow! That's got my mind working overtime. I wonder if any of the men were at the wedding. They might have seized the opportunity to put an end to his bullying once and for all."

"Maybe, who knows?"

"Actually, thinking about it, John Calshaw, James' former best friend, was away with the football team. I'm thinking the fathers would have travelled with the team."

"Good thinking."

"Louise, have you got that story ready yet?" a voice bellowed in the background.

"Crap, you'd better go, sweetie. Thanks for ringing. I hope you don't get into too much bother."

"I'll speak soon. He's a pussycat really, once he's torn into some raw meat at lunchtime." Louise laughed and hung up.

It was times like this that Ruth was grateful to be self-employed. Not having a boss breathing fire down her neck forty hours a week was a definite bonus.

She spent the rest of the afternoon writing down notes about the two different routes the investigation had taken so far.

Then she jotted down the questions that were puzzling her the most. Why did Bradley leave his own reception party? Why specifically go up to the turret and not simply take a walk around the garden if he'd wanted to seek out some quiet time away from the wedding furore? Had he found the whole day too much and killed himself, despite what Littlejohn thought? Or had someone tempted him up to the turret? Was he on a promise? On his damn wedding day?

She called James not long after she'd exhausted all the questions she was seeking answers to. He only added to her disappointment, telling her that the investigation had come to a grinding halt at his end.

Why didn't that surprise her? Inspector Littlejohn couldn't investigate a fart in a prune factory. She glanced up at the clock. It was four-thirty. Deciding she'd had enough for one day, she locked up the office and took Ben for a long walk down by the river to clear her head before going home for the evening. "Make the most of this walk, boy, it's your final one for the day. Once I get home tonight, I'm not budging from that couch." She cringed when she realised Carolyn and the boys would be there when she got home. "Oops, maybe I'll need to take a rain check on that one. Until James and I get our house back."

THE FOLLOWING DAY, back in the office, Ruth decided it was time she moved on to question the locals who ran several businesses in the area.

Her first stop was to Richard Knox who ran the local betting shop. She knew Richard well, not through frequenting his establishment, no, they had been friends since their schooldays. What he divulged absolutely floored her.

"I detested him, Ruth. He was a weasel. Actually, worse than that, an utter slimeball."

"I'm hearing that more and more as this investigation continues.

Why? What did he do in your eyes that warrants you thinking that, Richard?"

"In my line of business, you get to overhear what's going on in the community. I can tell by the expression on your face that has come as a surprise to you."

"Too right. Who'd have thunk it? And there was me thinking only women like to gossip."

He laughed and jabbed her in the ribs with his elbow. "You're a card, you are. We men don't *gossip*."

"No? What do you call it then?" she asked, perplexed, eager to understand the way men's minds worked, something that had evaded her over the years.

"We like to think of it as putting the world to rights."

"Whatever you like to call it, are you going to tell me what goss… snippets of information you overheard about Bradley?"

"Mostly about the way he disciplined the kids in the local football team. I heard that a couple of the boys' fathers took him aside one day to teach him a lesson and to get him to lighten up on their boys. But that's not all I've heard over the years. I also discovered that the women in this community consider him a bit of a sex pest."

"I've heard the same thing. Crikey, why didn't these people air their views publicly? Maybe Bradley might have mended his ways."

He scoffed. "I doubt that very much. Idiots like that never learn from their mistakes, not in my experience."

"Okay, I'm going to ask you something, and I think I already know what your answer is going to be, but I'll ask it anyway. Why did you go to the wedding on Saturday?"

"Because I couldn't let that girl down. Geraldine and I have always been close over the years. We dated when we were in school, don't you remember that?"

"I vaguely remember. What happened between you?"

He shrugged. "No idea. I think we simply drifted apart. She's a lovely girl, too bloomin' good for the likes of him."

"That's all I'm hearing during this investigation, and yet nobody ever plucked up the courage to tell Geraldine what he was truly like, including me."

"Maybe folks thought too much of her to do that. You know how fragile relationships can become where matters of the heart are concerned."

"Maybe. Gosh, I'm standing here thinking that all this could have been avoided if even half of what I've learned so far had come out in the open."

"You're her best friend. If you'd known something sooner, could you have told her?"

Ruth gulped and pulled a face. "The honest truth is, I don't know. What a terrible situation to be in, everyone in the community knowing what your other half was like, except you."

"I know, lass. We'll be here to support her going forward, she knows that."

"Glad to hear it. I have to ask if you noticed anything suspicious going on during either the wedding or the reception."

"I saw him, actually passed him on the stairs just before the incident happened."

Ruth's heart pounded against her ribs. "You did? Was he with anyone?"

"No. I asked him where he was going. He snarled at me and told me to mind my own business, if you must know."

"How strange. Did you see anyone else in the vicinity around that time? Someone he was possibly on his way to meet perhaps?"

He scratched his thinning hair and then lifted his specs, resting them on the top of his head as he thought. Then he clicked his thumb and forefinger together. "Come to think of it, I think I saw a flash of a black dress. Someone dashed across the landing at the top of the stairs. Gawd, don't quote me on that, it was the briefest glimpse, and I'd had a few on the day."

"Black dress, or do you mean black cloth? Could have it been a pair of pants you saw?"

"I don't know, maybe, although I'm inclined to believe it was a dress."

"So you didn't pass anyone when you were upstairs?"

"No. The only person I saw was Bradley on my way down. He was on his way up."

"Why were you up there?"

He looked over his shoulder to make sure no one was listening. "I was having a nose around the house at every opportunity. One of these days I'm going to earn enough off this place to buy a pad like that of my own. I wanted to know what to expect."

"Huge heating bills and maintenance costs is my bet, excuse the pun." She laughed at the look on his face. It was as if she'd swiped him around the cheek with a wet fish.

"Crikey, I never thought about the practicalities of running a big house."

"I doubt many people do. Stick to your comfortable semi and invest the money in a pension scheme. That way you'll be able to retire at sixty-five instead of what? Seventy-four? Isn't that what the damn limit is at the moment?"

"I think you're right. It's appalling. Don't worry, I've already got my pension in hand."

"Glad to hear it. I'd better get mine sorted out soon, we're not getting any younger, are we?"

"We're thirty-five, Ruth. I know I haven't got a foot in the grave yet, and I'm sure you haven't. Hey, are you ever going to marry James?"

"Why do you ask? More gossip you've been privy to that you'd like to enlighten me about?"

"No. Don't go biting my head off, you can see the man adores you. It's the wedding season, give the lad a chance."

"For a start, my love life is no concern of yours, and for another, I'm not ready for marriage. James is aware of that and has accepted it."

He lifted an eyebrow and tilted his head. "Has he?"

"If there's nothing else, I have other people I need to see, Richard," she replied stiffly, no hint of a smile on her face.

"Nope, nothing else. I didn't mean to offend, just telling it how I see it, love. Give your old man a break and let him slip that ring on your finger."

"Bye, Richard, thanks for the info…" She turned towards the door and called over her shoulder, "And the lecture."

"Hey, anytime, Ruth." His ridiculing laugh followed her out of the door.

So, someone was probably lying in wait for Bradley, but who? And why?

During her walk with Ben at the park, she had a brainwave. She fished out her phone and rang the station, asking to be patched through to James. He answered her call immediately.

"This is becoming a habit, Ruth, what do you want?"

She flinched at the tone of his voice. "Sorry, this will be the last time, I promise. I need you to do me a huge favour. Will you?"

"I'm hardly going to say yes if I don't know what you're going to ask me. What is it?"

Ruth chewed on her bottom lip. She feared he was going to go ballistic once he heard what she was calling about. "I need to see the crime scene photos."

"Like that's going to happen," he said, harsher than she'd anticipated.

She realised she was asking a lot. However, without those photos, she feared she would be going round and round for days to come. "Please, James. I've never asked this of you before, it's important. Look, if Littlejohn isn't coming up with the goods, then what harm can it do for me to see the photos? Pleeeeaaase?"

"Do you even care about getting me the sack?"

"Of course I do. It won't come to that."

"You're an idiot if you think that, Ruth."

"If you get the sack, I'll offer you a job. Hey, that's not a bad idea, come and work for me."

"That has to be the craziest idea you've had since the day I met you. What about my pension?"

"All right. It was a dumb idea, granted. How about it, James? There's a killer on the loose. That should be our priority."

"I can't."

"I know how difficult this could be for you, but please, I'm begging you. Something important has come to my attention, and I need to clarify things before I can announce who the killer is."

"You're talking to the wrong person. You need to speak to the inspector, not me."

"What? You know how much she hates me."

"I can see why at times," he grumbled. "All right, I'll see what I can do. No promises, though."

"You're amazing. I love you so much."

"Hah, only when you want something."

"I'm hurt you should say that."

"Liar. No, you're not. You're far too interested in the photos to be hurt."

"Thanks, James. I'll see you later. I'm going home soon."

"Part-timer. See you later."

There was a sudden spring in her step, and she raced around the field, chasing Ben. He barked excitedly, matching her own excitement.

JAMES WALKED in through the back door a few hours later. They had the house to themselves; Carolyn had insisted she should give them some space and had taken the boys out for a McDonald's and a movie.

Ruth sauntered sexily towards her man and flung her arms around his neck.

"You're so transparent, lady. I'm already aware that you've spotted a file in my hand."

She gasped and stepped away from him. "Gosh, so there is. How did I miss that?" She fluttered her eyelashes and grinned.

"Yeah, right. Do you want to see these before dinner or after?"

"I thought we'd have a takeaway for dinner, if you're up for it?"

"Yum, only if it's Chinese."

"Deal. Now let me see."

"I took a risk getting them, Ruth. In all seriousness, I've put my neck on the line for you. I need to get these back first thing before the inspector realises they're missing."

"Why didn't you use your camera instead of bringing the actual crime scene pics home? Never mind." She rolled her eyes. "I'm dying to see them. She wouldn't allow me up in the turret on the day."

James groaned, opened the file and spread the photos out on the table. They studied them one by one. Ruth gasped when she spotted what might be a vital clue in the fourth picture. "There. Look at that. Tell me what you see?"

James stared long and hard and eventually shook his head. "Nothing. What am I looking at?"

"The silver tray. That's it. I'm going back there tomorrow to question the staff again. I was there today and barely got a few words out of them. Someone knows more than they've let on. I intend to find out what that is."

"Be careful, Ruth. Why don't I pass on what you know to Inspector Littlejohn, let her and the team deal with it from here?"

"No way. I'm not going to let her bask in the glory. This is my case to solve. She's done precisely nothing up until now. Please, don't rob me of the satisfaction of rubbing her face in it again, James."

"All right. Now, let's have some dinner, and then you can show me how grateful you are."

CHAPTER 13

AFTER A RESTLESS NIGHT, Ruth showered, pulled on a pair of cropped beige trousers and a colour-coordinated T-shirt, washed down a piece of toast with a strong cup of coffee and raced out of the house, eager to begin her day after she'd walked Ben.

While she watched Ben chase the other dogs and the squirrels at the park, her mind was working overtime, wondering how she should approach Lady Falkirk about what she'd discovered.

Fifteen minutes later, she harnessed a panting Ben in the back seat and bit the bullet. She arrived at Carmel Cove Hall a few moments later. The place seemed deserted. No cars in the drive, no sign of life at all. *Damn! I should have called first.* She decided to take a chance and rang the bell anyway. It wasn't long before Mr Wells opened the door. His eyes narrowed for a fleeting second as he studied her.

"Miss Morgan, can I help?"

"Hello, Mr Wells. I'd like to see Lady Falkirk if it's all right? I know I should've called ahead but I was passing and thought I'd drop by on the off-chance."

He stepped out and pulled the door to behind him. "Lady Falkirk is expecting guests today. They should be arriving within the next hour or so. You'll have to come back another time, Miss Morgan."

"Sorry, that's not convenient for me. If you'd like to tell Lady Falkirk I'm here, I'm sure she'll accommodate me for a few minutes."

He sighed. "If you insist, I'll go and see if Lady Falkirk can spare the time." He left her standing on the doorstep.

Ruth waited until he dropped out of view then entered the hallway. A loud crash stopped her in her steps. Several people emerged from different areas off the hallway to see what the commotion was, one of them Lady Falkirk herself. "Oh my, what on earth?"

Belinda, who was walking through the hallway, had let slip a tray of drinks.

"Well, don't just stand there, girl, get this mess cleared up immediately. My guests are imminent. I want this place spotless for their arrival. Ruth, what are you doing here? Did you forget something yesterday?"

"Hello, Lady Falkirk. Something came to my attention last night, and I wondered if you had time for a brief chat." She turned to look at Belinda who was visibly shaking and appeared to be frozen in time. "Why did you drop the tray, Belinda?"

"I...umm...I'm sorry," she stuttered, her gaze darting between Lady Falkirk, Mr Wells and Ruth, settling on her father, as if pleading with him to intervene. Suddenly she bolted.

Ruth tried to go after her, but Mr Wells blocked her path.

"What is going on here, Wells?" Lady Falkirk demanded.

"You need to get out of my way, Mr Wells. I have a suspect to catch."

"Suspect? What do you mean, Ruth?" Lady Falkirk gasped as the truth dawned on her. "No. I don't believe it."

Ruth took a few steps to her left, trying to outfox Belinda's father, but he was wise and immediately cottoned on to what she was up to.

"Get out of her way, Wells. Whether she's your daughter or not, let Ruth do her job."

Wells's frame grew in stature, making it even harder for Ruth to get past him. Ruth had no other option than to stamp on the man's foot. He hopped around, and she slipped past him.

She was almost at the end of the hall when he shouted, "It wasn't her. It was me. I killed him."

"What? Killed who?" Lady Falkirk shrieked and then gasped as she seemed to register what was going on. Her mouth dropped open, and her gaze landed on Ruth.

Ruth was equally shocked by the revelation. She asked one question. "Why?"

The pain in his foot forgotten, Wells stood upright, although his shoulders drooped in resignation. "I'll tell you why, because he abused my daughter. The man was an animal. Someone had to intervene. He saw her on duty on Saturday. I caught him—he had her cornered in one of the rooms as she prepared the drinks. I entered the room, and he backed off. Belinda was a mess. She couldn't stop shaking. I couldn't let him get away with treating my daughter like that. I got her to drop a note in his pocket, asking him to meet Belinda upstairs in the turret. Of course, he jumped at the chance."

Ruth walked back towards him. "What? You're telling us you used your daughter as bait?"

"Not really. I would never have put her in that position. He thought he was going to meet her up there, but I took her place. Someone had to deal with him. The stories I've heard about him have been flying around town like no one's business."

"Why kill him? Why didn't you hand him in to the police?"

"It wasn't my intention to kill him. All I wanted to do was warn him off. Things got out of hand. Anyway, the police are run off their feet nowadays, they don't care. They're too busy 'chasing real criminals' not sex pests. Look how long that bloke who worked for the BBC got away with abusing sick people and the children he was supposed to be raising money for."

"Okay, I'll accept that, but why kill him?"

"I didn't mean to. He kept backing away from me while I was arguing with him. In the end he lost his footing and plunged to his death. You have to believe me, it was an accident."

The sound of gravel being torn up on the drive drew Ruth's attention. Flashing blue lights filled the hall. Ruth's heart sank when Inspector Littlejohn barged through the front door.

James must have told her, fearing that something might happen to me when I confronted the killer.

"I'll take it from here, Morgan," Littlejohn dismissed her abruptly.

Two uniformed officers stepped from behind the inspector and grabbed Wells. He didn't put up a fight. His gaze wandered to behind Ruth, and she turned to see Belinda standing there, tears streaming down her face.

"Please, it wasn't his fault. Don't arrest him."

"And you are?" Littlejohn demanded.

"She's his daughter. You'll need to take her in for questioning, too. In my eyes, they're both innocent," Ruth replied, her hackles up because of the way the inspector was speaking to everyone.

"I'll be the judge of that, Miss Morgan. You may leave now."

Ruth shook her head and grinned. "I'm here to see Lady Falkirk. I'm not going anywhere."

"Yes, yes, Ruth is my guest. I will not let you speak to her like that, Inspector. You have the suspects; you may leave my house now."

Seething, the inspector turned on her heel and exited the house with the two uniformed officers, Wells and his daughter, Belinda.

Ruth let out a huge sigh of relief once she and Lady Falkirk were alone. "Well, that was a shock."

"I should say so. What will happen to them both?" Lady Falkirk asked, appearing relieved as the pair of them crossed the hallway to the front door and watched the police cars drive off.

"I wouldn't like to say. Sorry to cause a disruption when you have guests arriving, Lady Falkirk."

She waved away the apology. "No problem. I don't suppose you know any unemployed butlers, do you? I fear I will be in need of one in the near future."

Ruth laughed. The tension that had gripped her shoulders moments earlier seeped away. "I'm sorry, I don't. I'd better go and break the news to Geraldine."

"Yes, yes, you must. Go quickly before she hears it from someone else." Lady Falkirk patted her on the back. "Well done, Ruth, for solving the mystery. One thing... What led you to believe that Belinda was involved in the crime?"

"Let's just say that something came into my possession last night that drew me back here. I didn't know Belinda or her father were involved until Wells confessed."

"Remarkable events. The whole affair has been quite unsettling for me."

"I can imagine. I'm sorry that the murder, or accident as Wells maintains the incident was, occurred on your doorstep."

"Thank you, dear, for being an excellent sleuth. I'll surely be recommending your services to my friends in the future, you can be certain of that."

Ruth shook her hand. "That, Lady Falkirk, would be extremely helpful in growing my business. Thank you."

"Now go and pass on the information to your dear friend."

"I will. I'll see you soon, no doubt."

RUTH SAT in the car outside Geraldine's house for several minutes before plucking up the courage to face her with the truth.

Geraldine opened the door, her faint smile slipping quickly when she saw Ruth's serious expression. "I'm not going to like this, am I?"

"Yes and no. I could do with a coffee. Are your parents around?"

"No. They went home yesterday. Come through to the kitchen." Geraldine shuddered and walked through to the small kitchen at the rear of her quaint terraced house.

Ruth held off starting the conversation until they were both sitting at the table. She reached across, placed her hand over Geraldine's and smiled. "The case has been solved, sweetie."

"You did it? I can't believe it, I thought it would never be solved. Who did it? Have they been arrested? What was their reason behind killing Bradley? Sorry, I'm bombarding you with questions."

"I can understand your eagerness. Let's start with who the guilty party is and work back from there. It was the butler."

Geraldine burst into laughter. "Stop messing about. This isn't a game of Cluedo or an Agatha Christie novel. Who really did it?"

Ruth inclined her head and nodded slowly. "It truly was the butler."

"Oh, goodness. Why?"

"Before I tell you, I need you to prepare yourself for what you're about to hear. It's not good news. I'd love to keep the information from you, but I think you have the right to know the type of man you married."

"Crap, I'm not liking the sound of that, Ruth."

"Neither did I when I learned the truth, I promise you. Where do I begin? Ah yes…are you aware that Bradley bullied the members of the local football team?"

"No. Are you sure?"

"Absolutely. I've spoken to several people over the past few days who have pointed the finger at him in that respect. That's the reason his best friend fell out with him, you know, John Calshaw."

"Never. Bradley told me that they'd simply drifted apart. I can't believe what you're telling me."

"That's only the tip of the iceberg, Geraldine." She picked up her mobile lying on the table beside her and flicked through the photos. She angled each one towards Geraldine before moving on to the next.

Geraldine frowned. "I don't understand, what am I supposed to be looking at?"

"The expressions on their faces, don't you see it, Geraldine?"

"They seem angry. Why? What were they looking at?"

"These photos were taken on Saturday, and each of the women were glaring at Bradley. That's a look of hatred, wouldn't you agree?"

"I suppose you're right. Why? I thought they all liked Bradley. This is news to me."

"I have a bigger blow coming up, brace yourself. Bradley either tried it on or abused each of these women."

Geraldine flung herself back in the chair. "What? I don't believe you. He wouldn't do such a thing."

"It's the truth. I had to force the information out of one or two of them, but their stories were basically the same. They also referred to him as being a sex pest."

"What? No way. Bradley was a pure gentleman."

"Maybe to you, Geraldine. My guess is that he was hiding very dark secrets from you. Who knows where that would have led to once your married life began?"

Geraldine shook her head in disbelief as Ruth continued to reveal the facts in all their glory.

"How did you find out it was the butler?" Geraldine finally asked after letting the truth settle for a moment or two.

"I asked James to get me the crime scene photos. I saw a silver tray in one of them, and Richard Knox mentioned he thought he saw a black dress cross the landing at the top of the stairs. I put two and two together, although I initially showed up at the Hall to question the staff again. It all kicked off when Belinda, the butler's daughter, saw me. She ran, I tried to chase her, and that's when her father admitted it was him."

"Are you sure he's not just saying that to protect his daughter?"

Ruth shrugged. "Maybe. It's up to the police to find out the truth now. I've done my bit."

Geraldine reached for her handbag and extracted her cheque book. "How much do I owe you?"

"Nothing. I told you this one was on me."

"No, I can't accept that. I employed you to find out who the culprit was."

"We'll discuss it later then, if you insist. Are you going to be okay?"

"I think so. I'll probably lock myself in the house for a few days, wallow in self-pity for the years I've wasted on that vile man, but I'll survive. I have to. Life goes on, right?"

"It does, love. We'll all be here to support you. Make sure you don't distance yourself from us."

She gasped. "What will happen about the funeral now? That's going to stick in my throat having to pay for it after all he's done wrong."

"Let me have a word with James, see what he can come up with. I'll get back to you later. Come on, give me a hug."

They left their seats, hugged each other and then parted.

Geraldine showed Ruth to the door. "I can't thank you enough for what you've done for me, Ruth. I'll never forget it."

"Hey, it was nothing. I know you'd do the same for me if the boot was ever on the other foot. My advice would be for you to forget about him now and get on with your life."

"I will, eventually."

EPILOGUE

OVER THE FOLLOWING MONTHS, life was frantic for Ruth and those around her. The Go Fund Me account reached a whopping eighty thousand pounds and enabled Carolyn, Keith and the boys to be in their home for Christmas, thanks to the expertise of a builder who had recently finished a large barn conversion in the next town. This meant James and Ruth got their house back to enjoy the festivities without having to feel obliged to care for Ruth's sister and her family.

For his part in helping to crack the case, James received a warning from his superiors, but then, so did the inspector for not treating the crime as an important one. She and her team were guilty of missing the one blatant clue that Ruth had spotted the instant the photos had come into her possession.

It took another three weeks before Geraldine plucked up the nerve to go ahead with the funeral. Unfortunately, the costs were indeed down to her in the end as the couple were legally married. She was initially annoyed but accepted the decision. However, the Am-Dram club put on a small show, and the proceeds went directly to Geraldine to help with the cost.

Once Bradley was six feet under, Geraldine made a declaration to all at his wake that she was back on the market and eager to get on with her life. Since the funeral, Geraldine had been on dozens of dates with numerous men, far too many for Ruth to keep up with.

The case came to court before Christmas. The biggest surprise of all was that twenty other women from the town came forward to give evidence relating to Bradley's shady past. Geraldine was once again beside herself, but Ruth sat alongside her throughout the proceedings. The judge took all the startling evidence into consideration when she passed down the sentences to Wells and his daughter. Wells was imprisoned for seven years for manslaughter, and Belinda was given a suspended sentence for perverting the course of justice because she knew her father had been present when Bradley had died. Whether it was deemed an accident in their eyes or not, she should have informed the police—she didn't.

In spite of the disruption to the town, the Am-Dram club put on one of their best shows the townsfolk had ever seen. *The Sound of Music* went down well with the locals, both young and old. In the end, it proved to be the feel-good factor for a town damaged by the truth.

THE END

NOTE TO YOU, THE READER.

Dear Reader,

Well that was a surprise outcome, wasn't it?

Ruth is a determined character, I hope you agree? Being up against her nemesis, DI Littlejohn makes her life tough at times.

Won't you come on another journey with Ruth and her group of trusted friends by grabbing a copy of MURDER AT THE HOTEL now?

As always, thank you for choosing to read my work from the millions of books available. If you wouldn't mind leaving a short review, or recommending my books to your family and friends, I'd be forever in your debt.

Until we meet again,

M A Comley

Printed in Poland
by Amazon Fulfillment
Poland Sp. z o.o., Wrocław

51239125R00115